The Children's Treasury of Virtues

EDITED BY
William J. Bennett
ILLUSTRATED BY
Michael Hague

SIMON & SCHUSTER
New York London Toronto Sydney Singapore

THE CHILDREN'S TREASURY OF VIRTUES

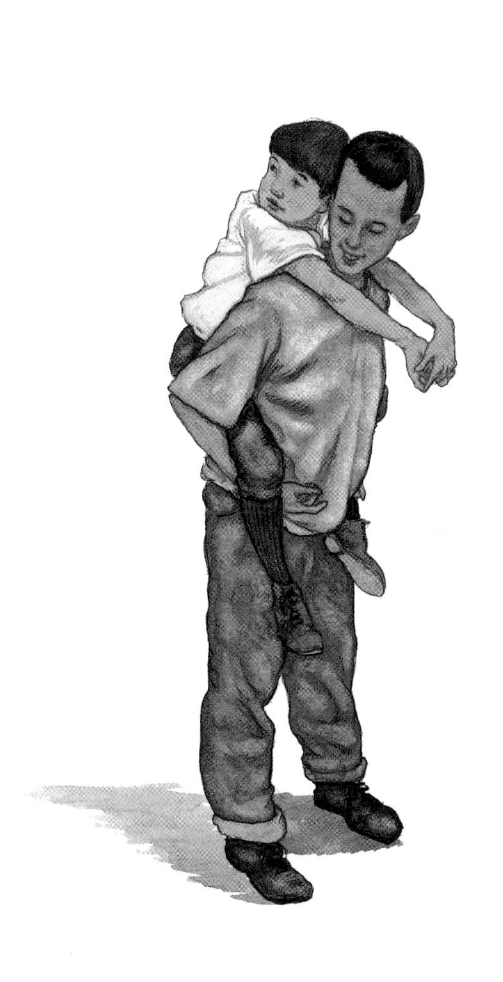

Simon & Schuster
Rockefeller Center
1230 Avenue of the Americas
New York, NY 10020

The Children's Book of Virtues and some portions of *The Children's Book of Heroes* are works of fiction. Names, characters, places, and incidents either are products of the author's imagination or are used fictitiously. Any resemblance to actual events or locales or persons, living or dead, is entirely coincidental.

Manufactured in the United States of America

10 9 8 7 6 5 4 3 2 1

Library of Congress Cataloging-in-Publication Data is available.

ISBN 0-7432-1136-7

These titles were previously published individually by Simon & Schuster.

CONTENTS

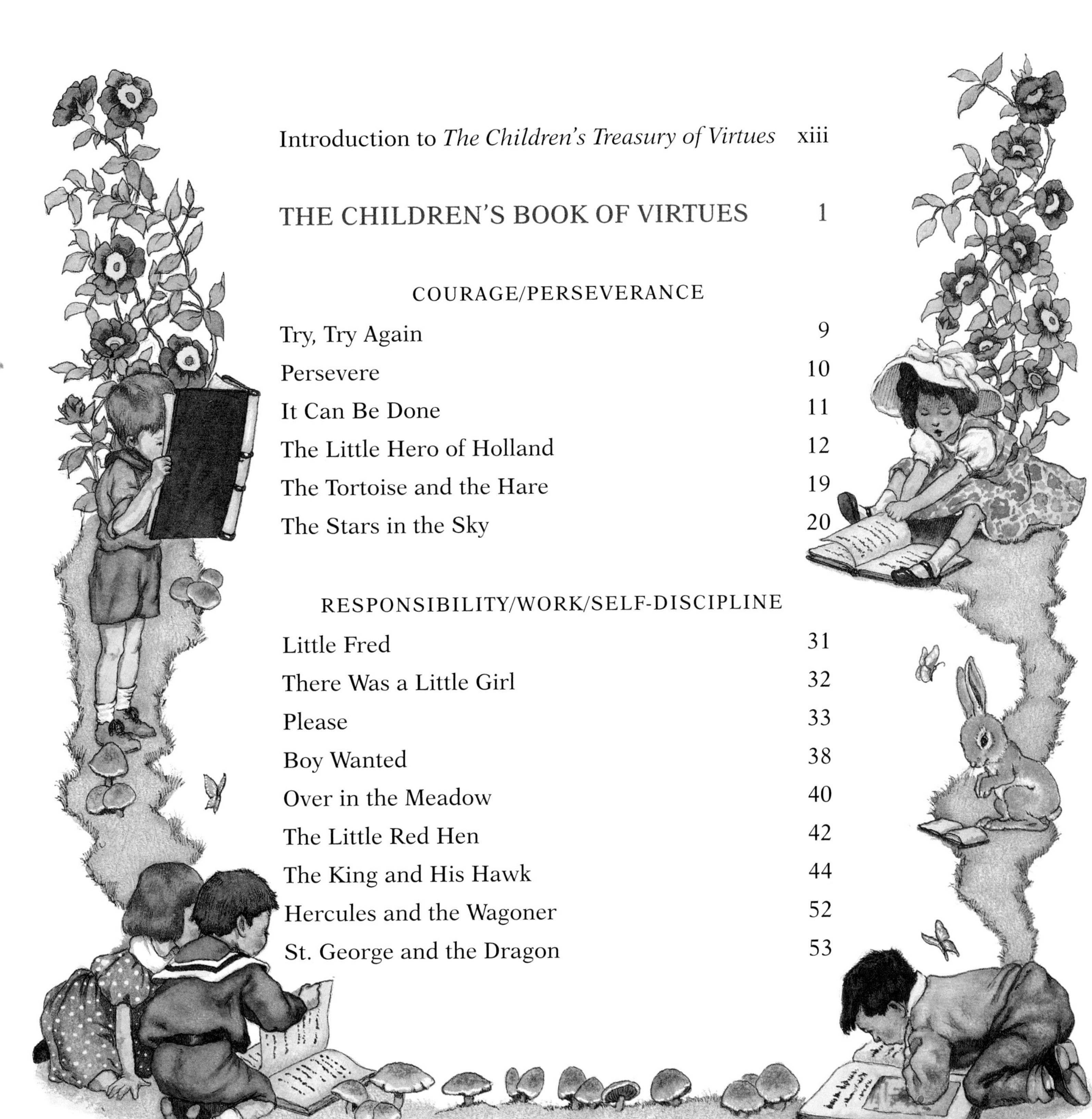

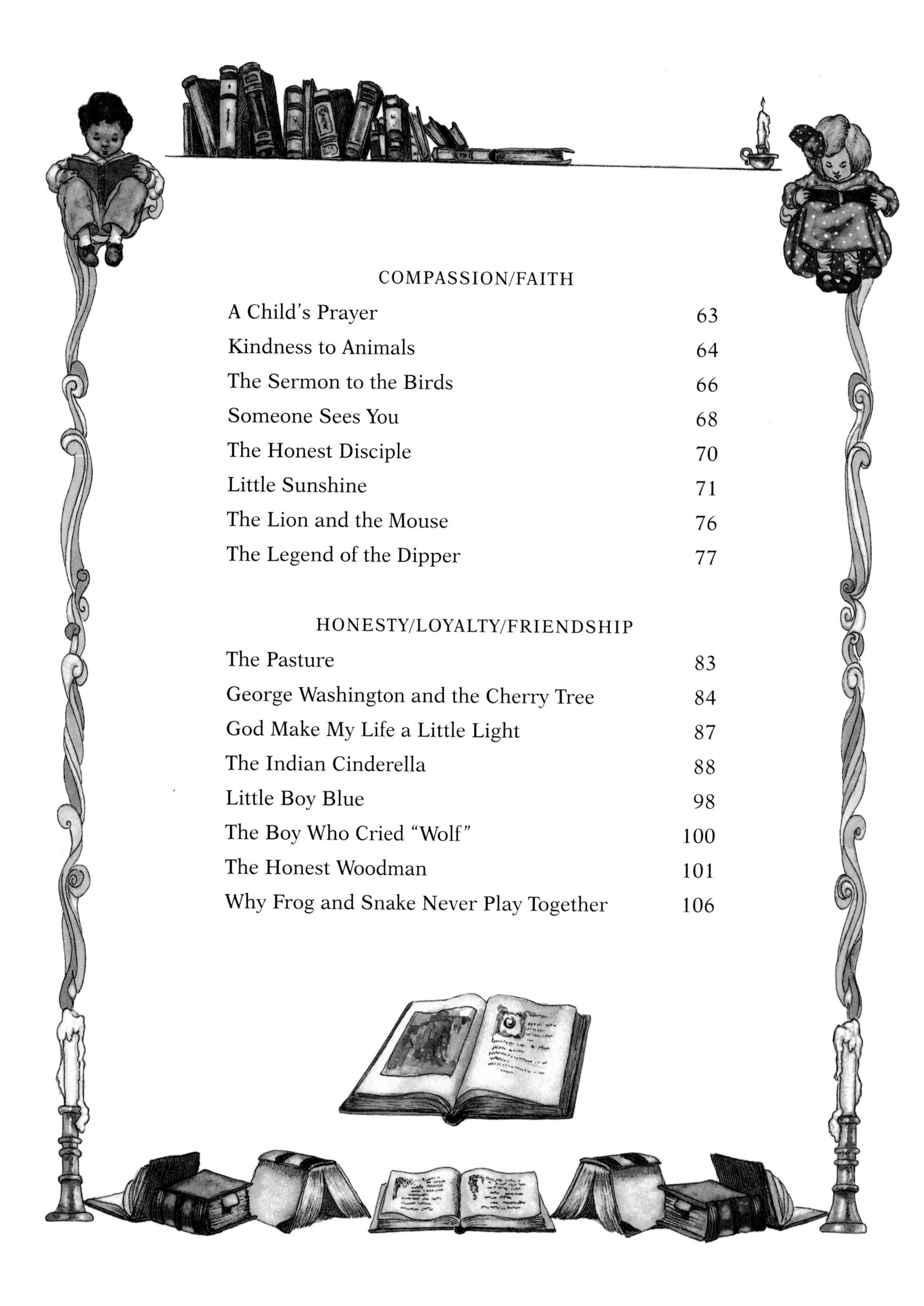

COMPASSION/FAITH

HONESTY/LOYALTY/FRIENDSHIP

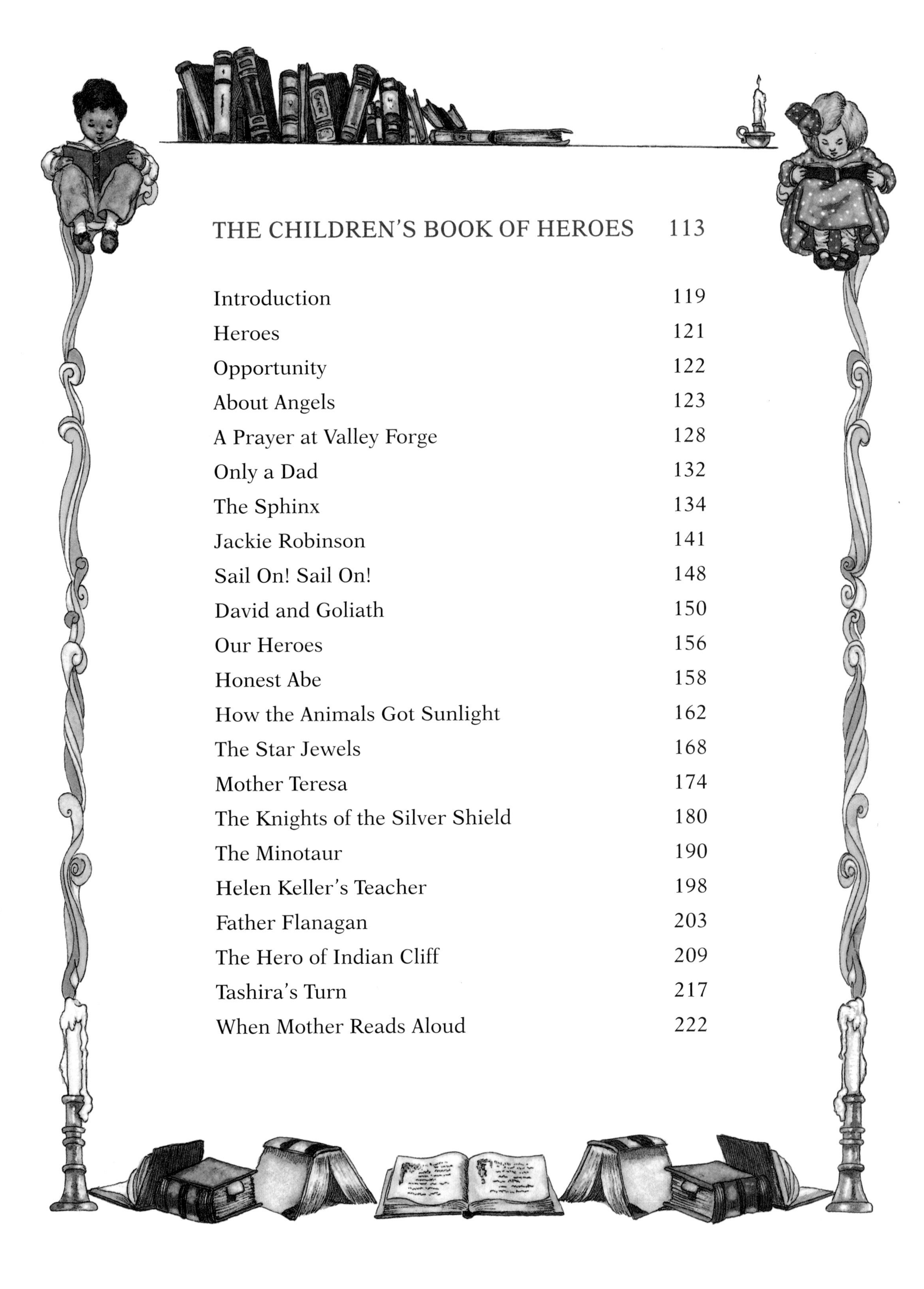

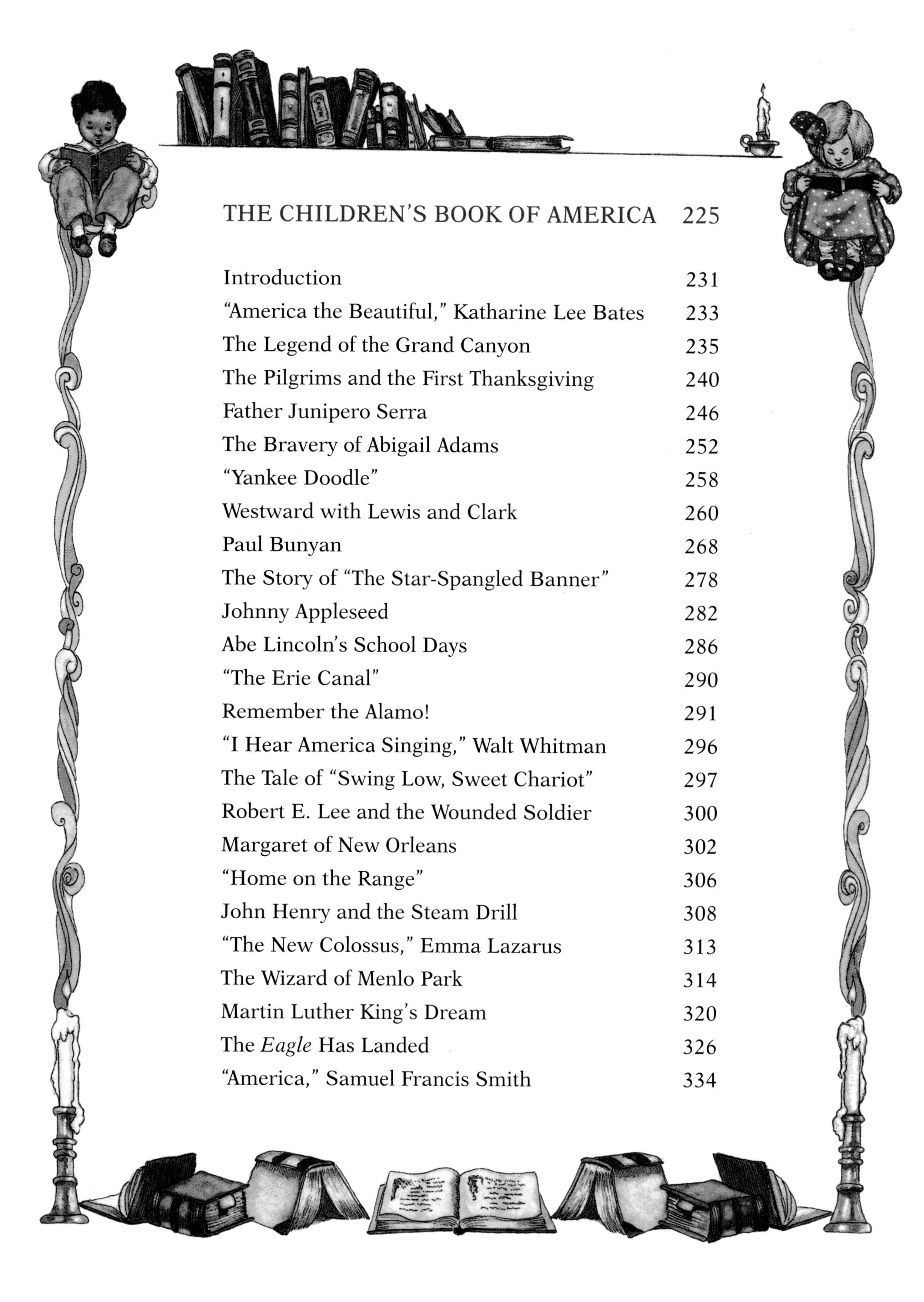

The Children's Treasury of Virtues

INTRODUCTION

THIS VOLUME COMBINES THE CONTENTS OF three previously published works whose common theme is training the heart and mind toward good things: good habits, good attitudes, good behavior. *The Children's Book of Virtues* helps teach what we might call moral literacy, that is, showing children what basic virtues look like, what they are in practice, and why they deserve our allegiance. *The Children's Book of Heroes* helps youngsters discern the kind of actions that merit imitation and the kind of individuals who deserve admiration. *The Children's Book of America* helps children learn about the ideals that democracy needs to flourish and the revered principles that make America great. All these goals are necessary for thorough character training in American homes and schools. So I was delighted when Simon & Schuster proposed bringing the stories and pictures of those three books together between two covers.

An old legend is worth bearing in mind as we think about raising children. The story tells of the ancient Greek hero Hercules, then a young man, coming to a fork in the road where two women stood. One woman, named Pleasure, told him that her road was smooth and pleasant, and led through flowery meadows where life had no toils or cares. The other woman, named Virtue, pointed to her road, which looked steeper and led toward high mountains. She said she could promise him nothing but what his own labor and strength would yield. Hercules chose the latter road, which turned out to be the path toward the heights of greatness.

That story may seem quaint to modern sensibilities. Some find it hard to believe that anyone would really choose the second road. Yet it is a good story, one that rings true, and one that is particularly fitting to our times. Today, the world in which our children live often encourages (or at least fails to discourage, which for children can be the same thing) attitudes that say, in effect, "anything goes," "do whatever feels right for you," and "you can have it all now." We don't want our children's lives to be one long, rough road, of course. But approaching life as a moral endeavor is not always a smooth and easy task. It is often the harder track. Virtues are not easily gained. They need constant practice and work. One of adults' most important tasks is to coax children onto the path of virtue.

It is crucial to begin that effort when children are young. "You know that the beginning is the most important part of any work," Plato reminded us, "especially in the case of a young and tender thing; for that is the time at which the character is being formed and the desired impression is more readily taken." The family is the first and most important incubator of morality. Home is where children come to know right and wrong through the protective care of those who love them more than anyone else. The character lessons youngsters learn in home, church, and earliest years of school will stay with them as they make their way through the world, and will determine to a large degree whether they live life well.

Sound character education is built in several ways. It comes by following rules of good behavior; by developing good habits through repeated practice; by following the examples of responsible adults; and by talking about the moral facts of life. The stories we share with young children are powerful allies. Even in an age of computer games and electronic toys, you can't beat a good story—especially when offered by a caring adult—for capturing a child's attention. Legends, folk tales, biographies, and poems can help youngsters learn what basic virtues are all about. They serve as reference points on a moral compass, giving children a clearer sense of direction in matters of right and wrong.

The selections in this volume, therefore, speak to children as moral and spiritual beings. Along with Michael Hague's brilliant illustrations, they fire imaginations and lift sights. They provide substance for youngsters in a time when so much that vies for their attention is vapid or even corrosive to the spirit.

Share these selections with your child, and I venture to predict that some will sink in and stick for a long time. One or two may even make a big difference in the years to come. More than a few men and women at a critical instant have recalled a simple fable, a familiar verse, or a childhood hero first encountered in the pages of a book. We can all use a little help when we come to those forks in the road of life. I hope this collection, in its own way, helps you set your child on the right path.

The Children's Book of Virtues

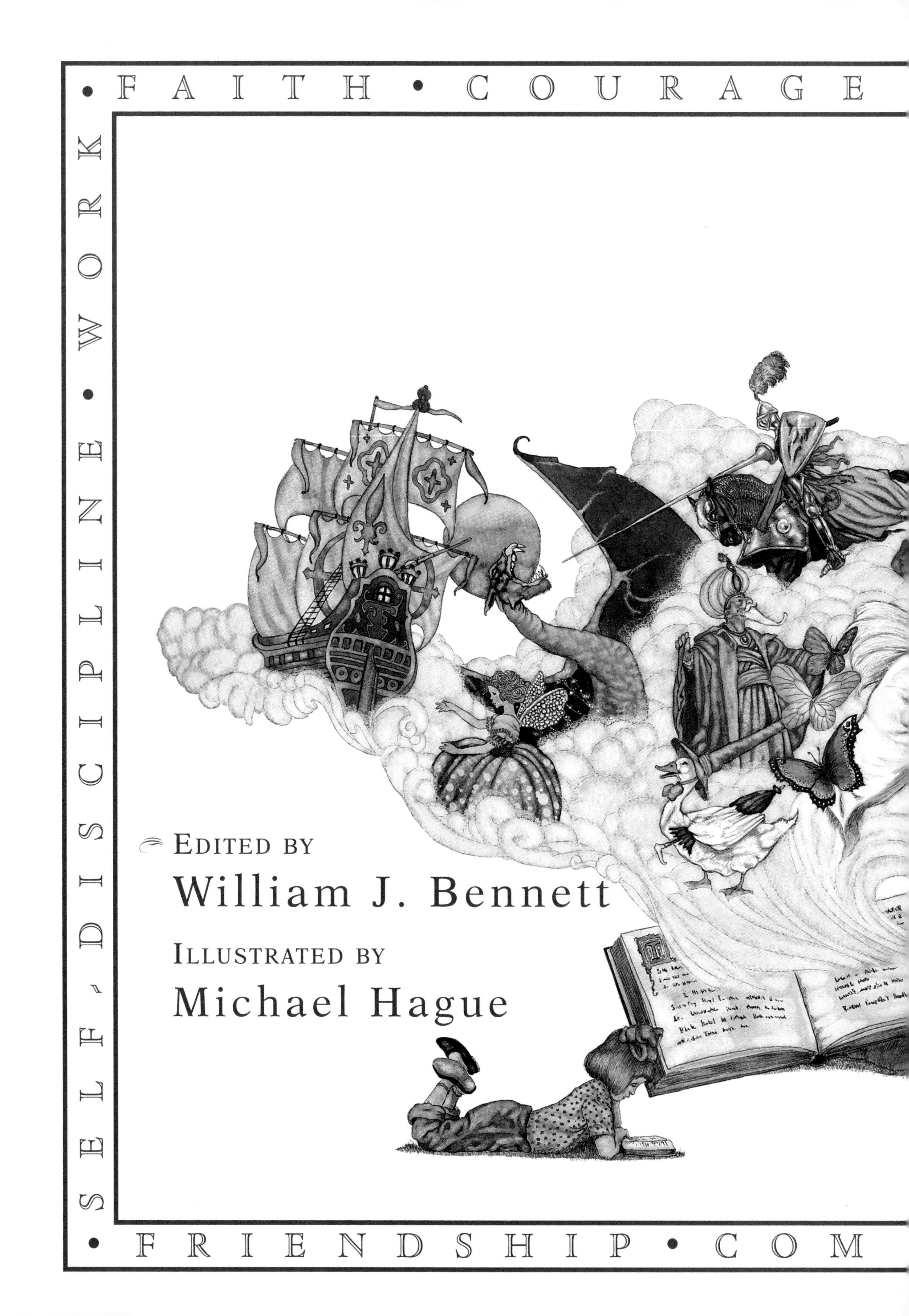

Edited by

William J. Bennett

Illustrated by

Michael Hague

RESPONSIBILITY • PERSEVERANCE • LOYALTY •

THE CHILDREN'S Book of Virtues

PASSION • HONESTY •

To my best blessings: Elayne, John, and Joseph.

—W.J.B.

Dedicated to the memory of a long-ago rainy afternoon with my picture books.

—M.H.

INTRODUCTION

The impetus for this book was a comment I began to hear over and over soon after the original *Book of Virtues* was published: "Our family loves these stories, but it's too bad there are no pictures!" As every parent knows, the chances of enticing a child to climb into (and stay in) your lap increase considerably when you hold out a picture book—as opposed to an eight-hundred-page anthology. So I was delighted when Simon & Schuster agreed to produce an illustrated edition of stories and poems selected from *The Book of Virtues* especially for younger children.

There was no question in my wife's mind as to who should paint the images to accompany these time-honored verses and tales. Elayne had passed more than a few story hours with our sons, John and Joe, at her side, reading books illustrated by Michael Hague. When I told her about this project, she reached for the phone and began tracking down her favorite illustrator. Fortunately, Michael was available and willing, and the happy results fill the following pages. As you will see, his images have a vital spark that leads young minds toward the noble and gentle and fine. Words and pictures speak together of hearts and souls where virtues dwell. These stories and Michael Hague's pen make a great match.

Like the original anthology, this edition aims specifically at the time-honored task of the moral education of the young. Moral education—the training of heart and mind toward the good—involves many things. It involves rules and precepts—the *do's* and *don'ts* of life with others. It involves explicit training in good habits. And it involves the example of adults who, through their daily behavior, show children they take morality seriously.

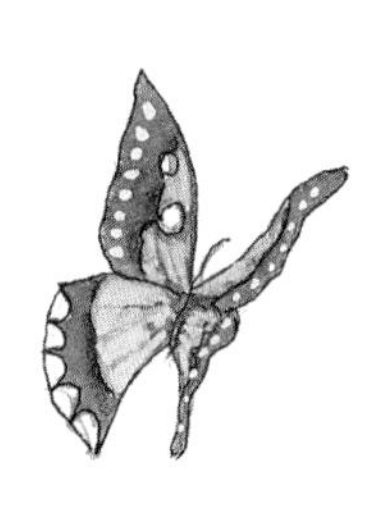

Along with precept, habit, and example, there is also the need for what we may call moral literacy. This collection is a "how to" book to help young children achieve such literacy. The stories and poems presented here can help them start to see what the virtues look like, what they are in practice, how to recognize them, and how they work. If we want our children to possess the traits of character we most admire—honesty and courage and compassion—we need to teach them what those traits are and why they deserve both admiration and allegiance.

It is never too early to begin the task. The stories in these pages can help build a first stock of examples illustrating what we perceive to be right or wrong, good or bad. They have stood the test of time in part because they are fascinating to young children. Nothing in recent years, on television or anywhere else, has improved on a good story that begins "Once upon a time . . ." But I believe they have stood the test of time for another reason. They appeal not only to children's imaginations but to their moral sense as well. They have the power to impress themselves upon young minds and remain as life-long guides.

And so the material in this book speaks without hesitation, without embarrassment, to the moral sense, to the souls of our children. Today we talk about how important it is to "have values," as if they were beads or a string of marbles in a pouch. But these stories speak to morality and virtues not as something to be possessed but as the core of human nature, not as something to *have* but as something to *be*, the most important thing to be. To dwell among these stories and verses is to put oneself, through the imagination, into a different place and time, a time when there was little doubt that children were essentially moral and spiritual beings, when the verities were the moral verities, when the central task of education was virtue. As we read these stories to and with our young children, we begin to acquaint them with the idea that it is the moral life, the life of virtue, that is worth living. We invite them to lift their young eyes. As St. Paul wrote, "Whatever is true, whatever is honorable, whatever is right, whatever is pure, whatever is lovely, whatever is of good repute, if there is any excellence and anything worthy of praise, let your mind dwell on these things."

I hope this book will help parents and young children dwell on these things together.

CONTENTS

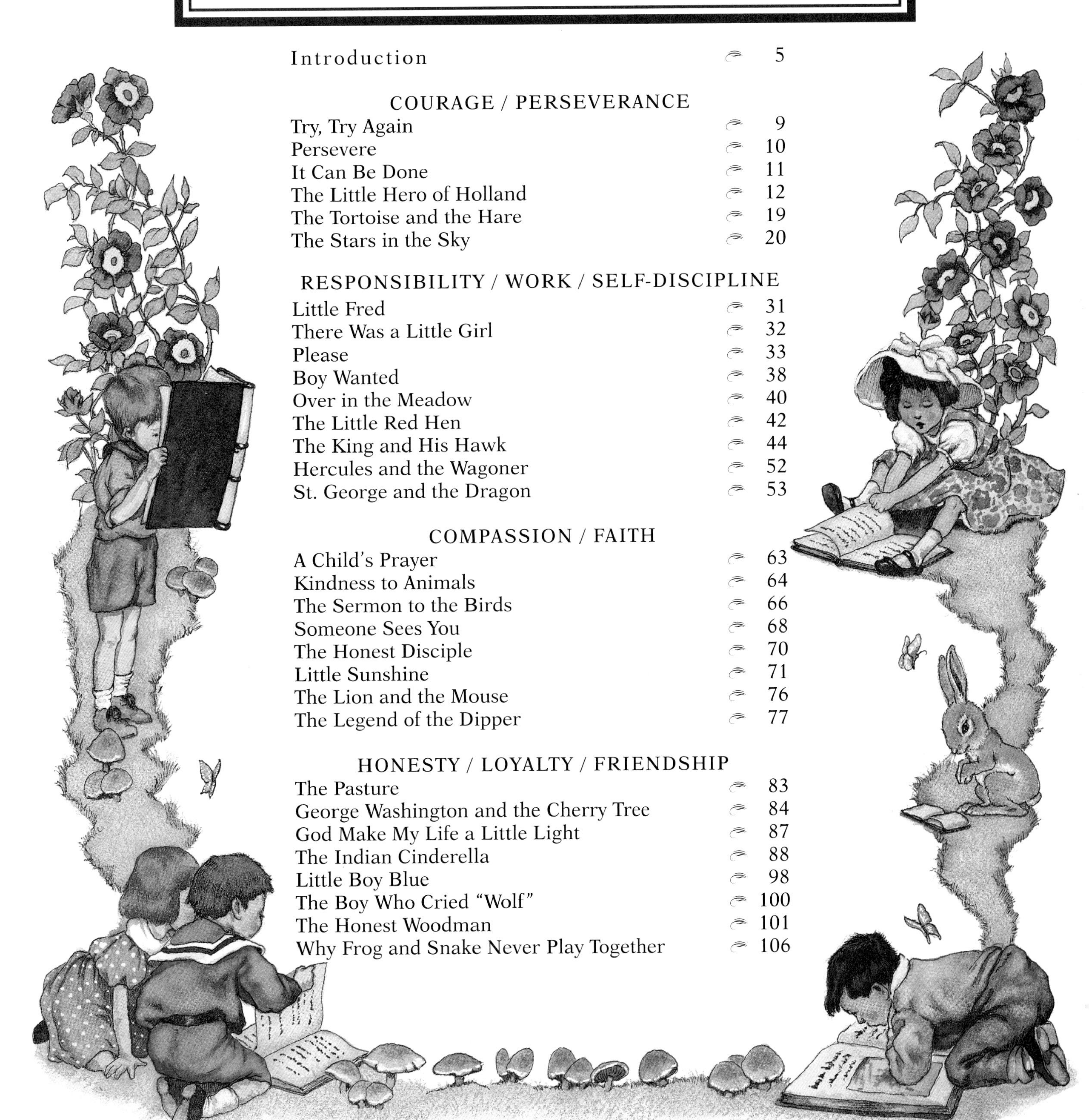

COURAGE
PERSEVERANCE

Try, Try Again

'Tis a lesson you should heed,
    Try, try again;
If at first you don't succeed,
    Try, try again;
Then your courage should appear,
For, if you will persevere,
You will conquer, never fear;
    Try, try again.

Persevere

Stick-to-it-iveness has a lot to do with getting the right answers in math, English, history, and life.

The fisher who draws in his net too soon,
    Won't have any fish to sell;
The child who shuts up his book too soon,
    Won't learn any lessons well.

If you would have your learning stay,
    Be patient—don't learn too fast;
The man who travels a mile each day,
    May get round the world at last.

It Can Be Done

Brave people think things through and ask, "Is this the best way to do this?" Cowards, on the other hand, always say, "It can't be done."

The man who misses all the fun
Is he who says, "It can't be done."
In solemn pride he stands aloof
And greets each venture with reproof.
Had he the power he'd efface
The history of the human race;
We'd have no radio or motor cars,
No streets lit by electric stars;
No telegraph nor telephone,
We'd linger in the age of stone.
The world would sleep if things were run
By men who say, "It can't be done."

The Little Hero of Holland

ADAPTED FROM ETTA AUSTIN BLAISDELL
AND MARY FRANCES BLAISDELL

Here is the true story of a brave heart, one willing to hold on as long as it takes to get the job done.

Holland is a country where much of the land lies below sea level. Only great walls called dikes keep the North Sea from rushing in and flooding the land. For centuries the people of Holland have worked to keep the walls strong so that their country will be safe and dry. Even the little children know the dikes must be watched every moment, and that a hole no larger than your finger can be a very dangerous thing.

Many years ago there lived in Holland a boy named Peter. Peter's father was one of the men who tended the gates in the dikes, called sluices. He opened and closed the sluices so that ships could pass out of Holland's canals into the great sea.

One afternoon in the early fall, when Peter was eight years old, his mother called him from his play. "Come, Peter," she said. "I want you to go across the dike and take these cakes to your friend, the blind man. If you go quickly, and do not stop to play, you will be home again before dark."

The little boy was glad to go on such an errand, and started off with a light heart. He stayed with the poor blind man a little while to tell him about his walk along the dike and about the sun and the flowers and the ships far out at sea. Then he remembered his mother's wish that he should return before dark and, bidding his friend good-bye, he set out for home.

As he walked beside the canal, he noticed how the rains had swollen the waters, and how they beat against the side of the dike, and he thought of his father's gates.

"I am glad they are so strong," he said to himself. "If they gave way what would become of us? These pretty fields would be covered with water. Father always calls them the 'angry waters.' I suppose he thinks they are angry at him for keeping them out so long."

As he walked along he sometimes stopped to pick the pretty blue flowers that grew beside the road, or to listen to the rabbits' soft tread as they rustled through the grass. But oftener he smiled as he thought of his visit to the poor blind man who had so few pleasures and was always so glad to see him.

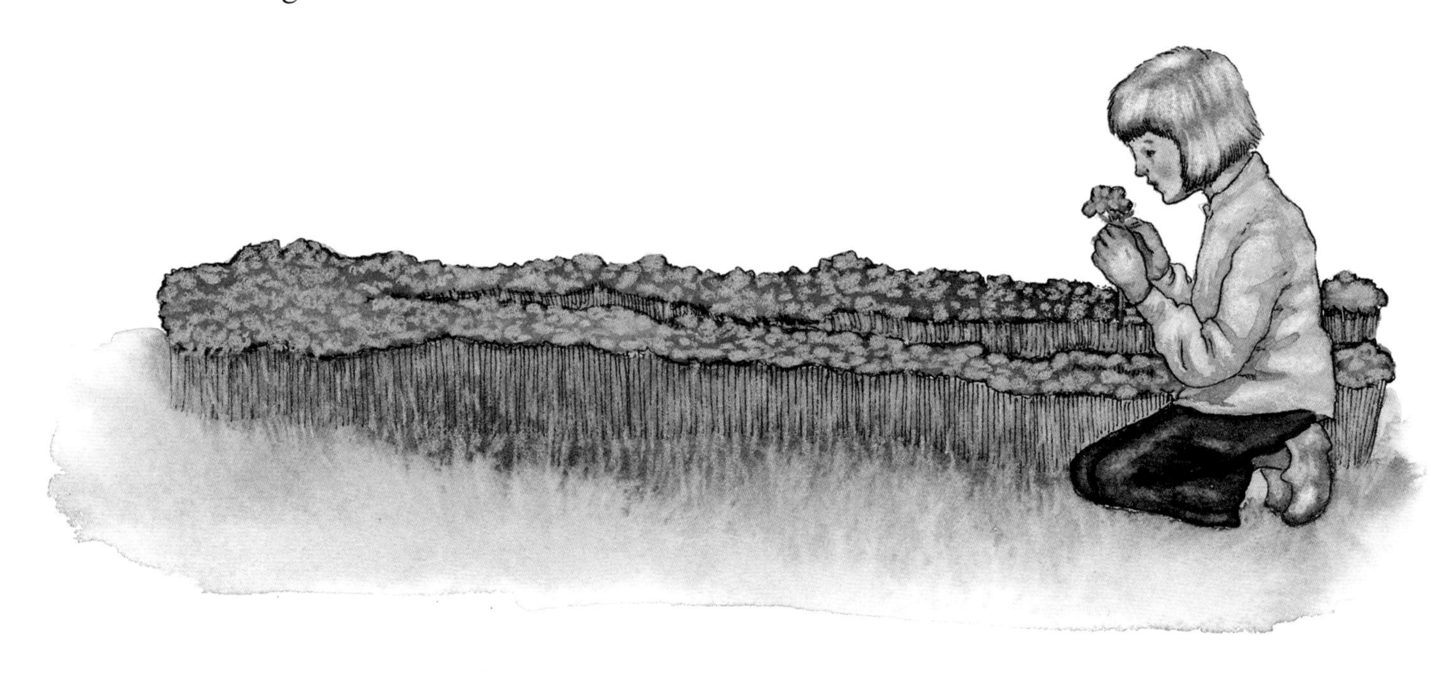

Suddenly he noticed that the sun was setting, and that it was growing dark. "Mother will be watching for me," he thought, and he began to run toward home.

Just then he heard a noise. It was the sound of trickling water! He stopped and looked down. There was a small hole in the dike, through which a tiny stream was flowing.

Any child in Holland is frightened at the thought of a leak in the dike.

Peter understood the danger at once. If the water ran through a little hole it would soon make a larger one, and the whole country would be flooded. In a moment he saw what he must do. Throwing away his flowers, he climbed down the side of the dike and thrust his finger into the tiny hole.

The flowing of the water was stopped!

"Oho!" he said to himself. "The angry waters must stay back now. I can keep them back with my finger. Holland shall not be drowned while I am here."

This was all very well at first, but it soon grew dark and cold. The little fellow shouted and screamed. "Come here; come here," he called. But no one heard him; no one came to help him.

It grew still colder, and his arm ached, and began to grow stiff and numb. He shouted again, "Will no one come? Mother! Mother!"

But his mother had looked anxiously along the dike road many times since sunset for her little boy, and now she had closed and locked the cottage door, thinking that Peter was spending the night with his blind friend, and that she would scold him in the morning for staying away from home without her permission.

Peter tried to whistle, but his teeth chattered with the

cold. He thought of his brother and sister in their warm beds, and of his dear father and mother. "I must not let them be drowned," he thought. "I must stay here until someone comes, if I have to stay all night."

The moon and stars looked down on the child crouching on a stone on the side of the dike. His head was bent, and his eyes were closed, but he was not asleep, for every now and then he rubbed the hand that was holding back the angry sea.

"I'll stand it somehow," he thought. So he stayed there all night keeping the water out.

Early the next morning a man going to work thought he heard a groan as he walked along the top of the dike. Looking over the edge, he saw a child clinging to the side of the great wall.

"What's the matter?" he called. "Are you hurt?"

"I'm keeping the water back!" Peter yelled. "Tell them to come quickly!"

The alarm was spread. People came running with shovels, and the hole was soon mended.

They carried Peter home to his parents, and before long the whole town knew how he had saved their lives that night. To this day, they have never forgotten the brave little hero of Holland.

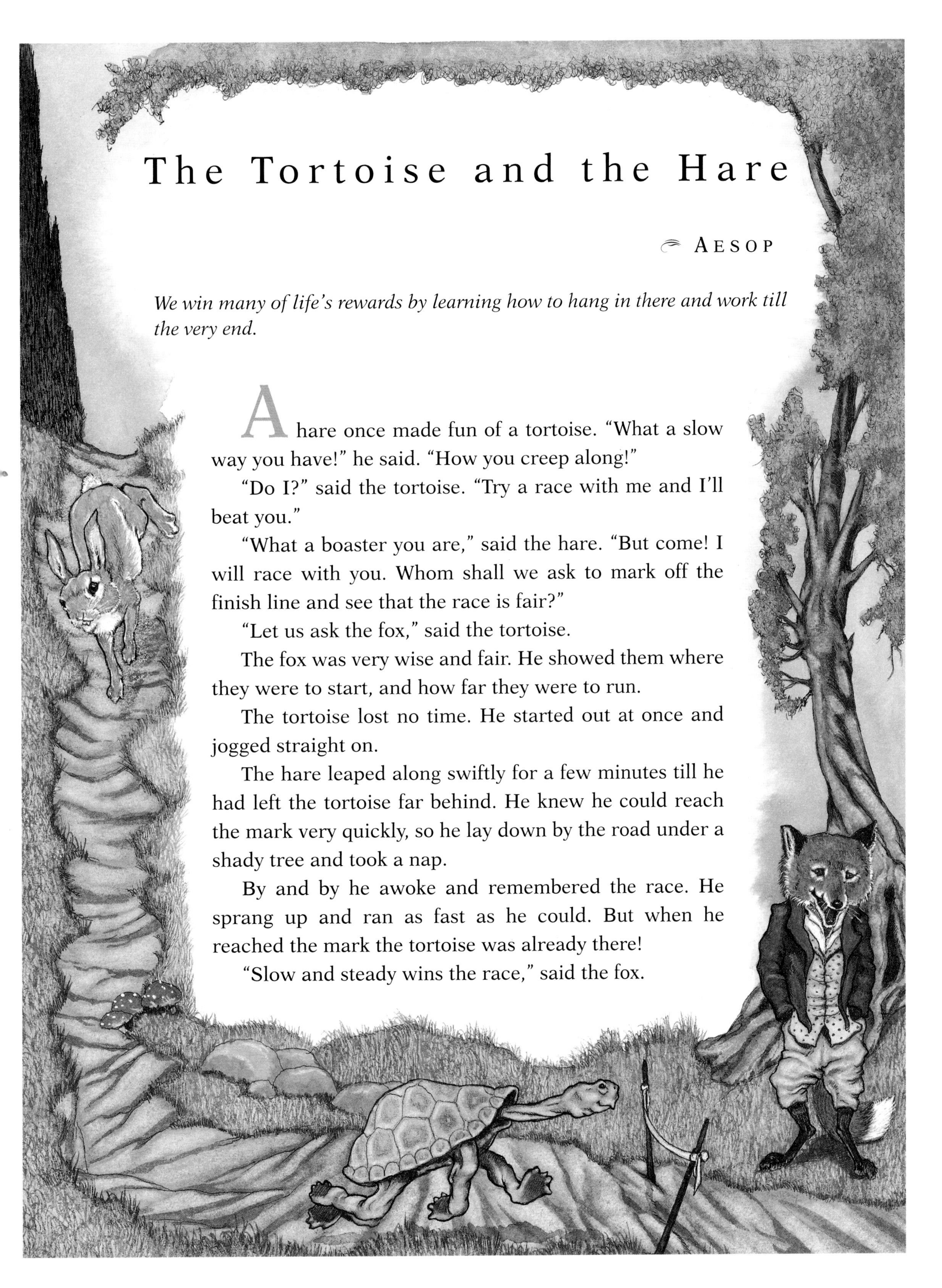

The Tortoise and the Hare

AESOP

We win many of life's rewards by learning how to hang in there and work till the very end.

A hare once made fun of a tortoise. "What a slow way you have!" he said. "How you creep along!"

"Do I?" said the tortoise. "Try a race with me and I'll beat you."

"What a boaster you are," said the hare. "But come! I will race with you. Whom shall we ask to mark off the finish line and see that the race is fair?"

"Let us ask the fox," said the tortoise.

The fox was very wise and fair. He showed them where they were to start, and how far they were to run.

The tortoise lost no time. He started out at once and jogged straight on.

The hare leaped along swiftly for a few minutes till he had left the tortoise far behind. He knew he could reach the mark very quickly, so he lay down by the road under a shady tree and took a nap.

By and by he awoke and remembered the race. He sprang up and ran as fast as he could. But when he reached the mark the tortoise was already there!

"Slow and steady wins the race," said the fox.

The Stars in the Sky

ADAPTED FROM CAROLYN SHERWIN BAILEY, KATE DOUGLAS WIGGIN, AND NORA ARCHIBALD SMITH

This old English tale reminds us that the higher we reach, the longer and harder we have to try.

Once upon a time there was a little lass who wanted nothing more than to touch the stars in the sky. On clear, moonless nights she would lean out her bedroom window, gazing up at the thousand tiny lights scattered across the heavens, wondering what it would be like to hold one in her hand.

One warm summer evening, a night when the Milky

Way shone more brightly than ever before, she decided she couldn't stand it any longer—she just had to touch a star or two, no matter what. So she slipped out the window and started off by herself to see if she could reach them.

She walked a long, long time, and then farther still, until she came to a mill wheel, creaking and grinding away.

"Good evening," she said to the mill wheel. "I would like to play with the stars in the sky. Have you seen any near here?"

"Ah, yes," groaned the old mill wheel. "Every night they shine in my face from the surface of this pond until I cannot sleep. Jump in, my lass, and you will find them."

The little girl jumped into the pond and swam around until her arms were so tired she could swim no longer, but she could not find any stars.

"Excuse me," she called to the old mill wheel, "but I don't believe there are any stars here after all!"

“Well, there certainly were before you jumped in and stirred the water up,” the mill wheel called back. So she climbed out and dried herself off as best she could, and set out again across the fields.

After a while she sat down to rest in a meadow, and it must have been a fairy meadow, because before she knew it a hundred little fairies came scampering out to dance on the grass.

"Good evening, Little Folk," said the girl. "I'm trying to reach the stars in the sky. Have you seen any near here?"

"Ah, yes," sang the fairies. "They glisten every night among the blades of grass. Come and dance with us, little lass, and you will find as many stars as you like."

So the child danced and danced, she whirled round and round in a ring with the Little Folk, but though the grass gleamed beneath her feet, she never spied a single star. Finally she could dance no longer, and she plopped down inside the ring of fairies.

"I've tried and I've tried, but I can't seem to reach the stars down here," she cried. "If you don't help me, I'll never find any to play with."

The fairies all whispered together. Finally one of them crept up and took her by the hand, and said: "If you're really determined, you must go forward. Keep going forward, and mind you take the right road. Ask Four Feet to carry you to No Feet At All, and then tell No Feet At All to carry you to the Stairs Without Steps, and if you climb that—"

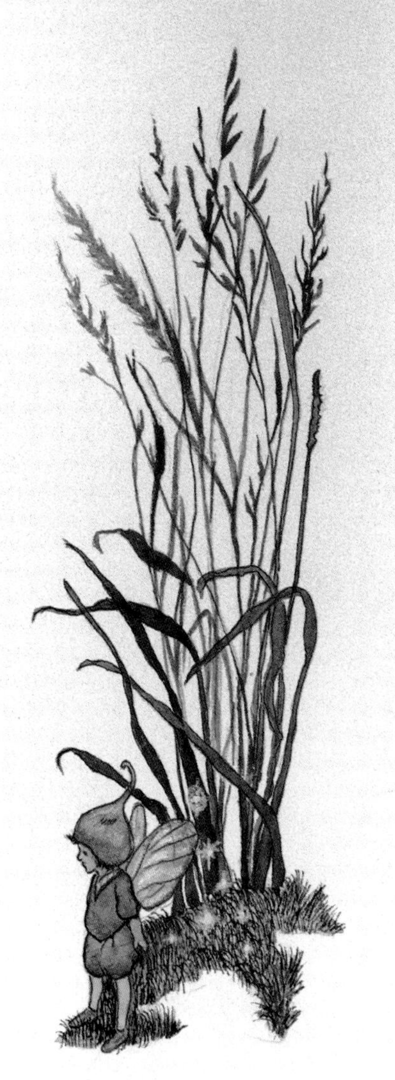

So the little girl set out again with a light heart, and by and by she came to a horse, tied to a tree.

"Good evening," she said. "I'm trying to reach the stars in the sky, and I've come so far my bones are aching. Will you give me a ride?"

"I don't know anything about stars in the sky," the horse replied. "I'm here only to do the bidding of the Little Folk."

"But I come from the Little Folk, and they said to tell Four Feet to carry me to No Feet At All."

"Four Feet? That's me!" the horse whinnied. "Jump up and ride with me."

They rode and they rode and they rode, till they rode out of the forest and found themselves at the edge of the sea.

"I've brought you to the end of the land, and that's as much as Four Feet can do," said the horse. "Now I must get home to my own folk."

So the little girl slid down and walked along the sea, wondering what in the world she would do next, until suddenly the biggest fish she'd ever seen came swimming up to her feet.

"Good evening," she said to the fish. "I'm trying to reach the stars in the sky. Can you help me?"

"I'm afraid I can't," gurgled the fish, "unless, of course, you bring me word from the Little Folk."

"But I do," she cried. "They said Four Feet would bring me to No Feet At All, and then No Feet At All would carry me to the Stairs Without Steps."

"Ah, well," said the fish, "that's all right then. Get on my back and hold on tight."

And off he went—kerplash!—into the water, swimming along a silver path that glistened on the surface and seemed to stretch toward the end of the sea, where the water met the sky. There, in the distance, the little girl saw a beautiful rainbow rising out of the ocean and into the heavens, shining with all the colors.

At last they came to the foot of it, and she saw the rainbow was really a broad bright road, sloping up and away into the sky, and at the far, far end of it she could see wee shining things dancing about.

"I can go no farther," said the fish. "Here are the Stairs Without Steps. Climb up, if you can, but hold on tight. These stairs were never meant for little lassies' feet, you know." So the little girl jumped off No Feet's back, and off he splashed through the water.

She climbed and she climbed and she climbed up the rainbow. It wasn't easy. Every time she took one step, she seemed to slide back two. And even though she climbed until the sea was far below, the stars in the sky looked farther away than ever.

"But I won't give up," she told herself. "I've come so far, I can't go back."

Up and up she went. The air grew colder and colder, but the sky turned brighter and brighter, and finally she could tell she was nearing the stars.

"I'm almost there!" she cried.

And sure enough, suddenly she reached the very tiptop of the rainbow. Everywhere she looked, the stars were turning and dancing. They raced up and down, and back and forth, and spun in a thousand colors around her.

"I'm finally here," she whispered to herself. She had never seen anything so beautiful before, and she stood gazing and wondering at the heavens.

But after a while she realized she was shivering with cold, and when she looked down into the darkness, she could no longer see the earth. She wondered where her own home was, so far away, but no streetlamps or window lights marked the blackness below. She began to feel a little dizzy.

"I won't go until I touch one star," she told herself, and she stood on her toes and stretched her arms as high as she could. She reached farther and farther—and suddenly a shooting star zipped by and surprised her so much she lost her balance.

Down she slid—down—down—down the rainbow. The farther she slid, the warmer it grew, and the warmer it grew, the sleepier she felt. She gave a great yawn, and a small sigh, and before she knew it, she was fast asleep.

When she woke up, she found herself in her very own bed. The sun was peeking through her window, and the morning birds sang in the bushes and trees.

"Did I really touch the stars?" she asked herself. "Or was it only a dream?"

Then she felt something in her hand. When she opened her fist, a tiny light flashed in her palm, and at once was gone, and she smiled because she knew it was a speck of stardust.

RESPONSIBILITY • WORK • SELF-DISCIPLINE

Little Fred

In which we learn how to retire for the evening.

When little Fred
  Was called to bed,
He always acted right;
  He kissed Mama,
  And then Papa,
And wished them all good night.

  He made no noise,
  Like naughty boys,
But gently up the stairs
  Directly went,
  When he was sent,
And always said his prayers.

There Was a Little Girl

In this poem, we see what happens to us sometimes when we do not behave!

There was a little girl,
And she had a little curl
Right in the middle of her forehead.
When she was good
She was very, very good,
And when she was bad she was horrid.

One day she went upstairs,
When her parents, unawares,
In the kitchen were occupied with meals,
And she stood upon her head
In her little trundle-bed,
And then began hooraying with her heels.

Her mother heard the noise,
And she thought it was the boys
A-playing at a combat in the attic;
But when she climbed the stair,
And found Jemima there,
She took and she did scold her most emphatic.

PLEASE

ALICIA ASPINWALL

Good children learn good manners (sometimes from their brothers and sisters).

There was once a little word named "Please" that lived in a small boy's mouth. Pleases live in everybody's mouth, though people often forget they are there.

Now, all Pleases, to be kept strong and happy, should be taken out of the mouth very often, so they can get air. They are like little fish in a bowl, you know, that come popping up to the top of the water to breathe.

The Please I am going to tell you about lived in the mouth of a boy named Dick; but only once in a long while did it have a chance to get out. For Dick, I am sorry to say, was a rude little boy; he hardly ever remembered to say "Please."

"Give me some bread! I want some water! Give me that book!"—that is the way he would ask for things.

His father and mother felt very bad about this. And as for the poor Please itself, it would sit up on the roof of the boy's mouth day after day, hoping for a chance to get out. It was growing weaker and weaker every day.

This boy Dick had a brother, John. Now, John was older than Dick—he was almost ten; and he was just as polite as Dick was rude. So his Please had plenty of fresh air, and was strong and happy.

One day at breakfast, Dick's Please felt that he must have some fresh air, even if he had to run away. So out he ran—out of Dick's mouth—and took a long breath. Then he crept across the table and jumped into John's mouth!

The Please-who-lived-there was very angry.

"Get out!" he cried. "You don't belong here! This is *my* mouth!"

"I know it," replied Dick's Please. "I live over there in that brother's mouth. But alas! I am not happy there. I am never used. I never get a breath of fresh air! I thought you might be willing to let me stay here for a day or so—until I felt stronger."

"Why, certainly," said the other Please, kindly. "I understand. Stay, of course; and when my master uses me, we will both go out together. He is kind, and I am sure he would not mind saying 'Please' twice. Stay as long as you like."

That noon, at dinner, John wanted some butter; and this is what he said:

"Father, will you pass me the butter, please—please?"

"Certainly," said the father. "But why be so *very* polite?"

John did not answer. He was turning to his mother, and said, "Mother, will you give me a muffin, please—please?"

His mother laughed.

"You shall have the muffin, dear; but why do you say 'please' twice?"

"I don't know," answered John. "The words seem just to jump out, somehow. Katie, please—please, some water!"

This time, John was almost frightened.

"Well, well," said his father, "there is no harm done. One can't be too 'pleasing' in this world."

All this time little Dick had been calling, "Give me an egg! I want some milk. Give me a spoon!" in the rude way he had. But now he stopped and listened to his brother. He thought it would be fun to try to talk like John; so he began, "Mother, will you give me a muffin, m-m-m-?"

He was trying to say "please," but how could he? He

never guessed that his own little Please was sitting in John's mouth. So he tried again, and asked for the butter.

"Mother, will you pass me the butter, m-m-m-?"

That was all he could say.

So it went on all day, and everyone wondered what was the matter with those two boys. When night came, they were both so tired, and Dick was so cross, that their mother sent them to bed very early.

But the next morning, no sooner had they sat down to breakfast than Dick's Please ran home again. He had had so much fresh air the day before that now he was feeling quite strong and happy. And the very next moment, he had another airing, for Dick said, "Father, will you cut my orange, please?" Why! the word slipped out as easily as could be! It sounded just as well as when John said it—John was saying only one "please" this morning. And from that time on, little Dick was just as polite as his brother.

Boy Wanted

FRANK CRANE

This "want ad" appeared in the early part of this century.

WANTED–A boy who stands straight, sits straight, acts straight and talks straight;

A boy whose fingernails are not in mourning, whose ears are clean, whose shoes are polished, whose clothes are brushed, whose hair is combed, and whose teeth are well cared for;

A boy who listens carefully when he is spoken to, who asks questions when he does not understand, and does not ask questions about things that are none of his business;

A boy who moves quickly and makes as little noise about it as possible;

A boy who whistles in the street, but does not whistle where he ought to keep still;

A boy who looks cheerful, has a ready smile for everybody, and never sulks;

A boy who is polite to every man and respectful to every woman and girl;

A boy who does not smoke cigarettes and has no desire to learn how;

A boy who is more eager to know how to speak good English than to talk slang;

A boy who neither bullies other boys nor allows other boys to bully him;

A boy who, when he does not know a thing, says, "I don't know," and when he has made a mistake says, "I'm sorry," and when he is asked to do a thing says, "I'll try";

A boy who looks you right in the eye and tells the truth every time;

A boy who is eager to read good books;

A boy who would rather put in his spare time at the YMCA gymnasium than gamble for pennies in a back room;

A boy who does not want to be "smart" or in any wise to attract attention;

A boy who would rather lose his job or be expelled from school than tell a lie or be a cad;

A boy whom other boys like;

A boy who is at ease in the company of girls;

A boy who is not sorry for himself, and not forever thinking and talking about himself;

A boy who is friendly with his mother, and more intimate with her than anyone else;

A boy who makes you feel good when he is around;

A boy who is not goody-goody, a prig, or a little pharisee, but just healthy, happy, and full of life.

This boy is wanted everywhere. The family wants him, the school wants him, the office wants him, the boys want him, the girls want him, all creation wants him.

Over in the Meadow

OLIVE A. WADSWORTH

Parents show responsibility by caring for their children. Children show responsibility by listening to their parents.

Over in the meadow,
In the sand, in the sun,
Lived an old mother toad
And her little toadie one.
"Wink," said the mother;
"I wink," said the one;
So she winked and she blinked
In the sand, in the sun.

Over in the meadow,
Where the stream runs blue,
Lived an old mother fish
And her little fishes two.
"Swim," said the mother;
"We swim," said the two;
So they swam and they leaped
Where the stream runs blue.

Over in the meadow,
In a hole in a tree,
Lived an old mother bluebird
And her little birdies three.
"Sing," said the mother;
"We sing," said the three;
So they sang and were glad,
In the hole in the tree.

Over in the meadow,
In the reeds on the shore,
Lived a mother muskrat
And her little ratties four.
"Dive," said the mother;
"We dive," said the four;
So they dived and they burrowed
In the reeds on the shore.

The Little Red Hen

RETOLD BY PENRYHN W. COUSSENS

If we want a share of the rewards, we must take a share of the work, too.

A little red hen once found a grain of wheat. "Who will plant this wheat?" she says.

"I won't," says the dog.

"I won't," says the cat.

"I won't," says the pig.

"I won't," says the turkey.

"Then I will," says the little red hen. "Cluck! cluck!"

So she planted the grain of wheat. Very soon the wheat began to grow and the green leaves came out of the ground. The sun shone and the rain fell and the wheat kept on growing until it was tall, strong, and ripe.

"Who will reap this wheat?" says the little red hen.

"I won't," says the dog.

"I won't," says the cat.

"I won't," says the pig.

"I won't," says the turkey.

"I will, then," says the little red hen. "Cluck! cluck!"

So she reaped the wheat.

"Who will thresh this wheat?" says the little red hen.

"I won't," says the dog.

"I won't," says the cat.

"I won't," says the pig.

"I won't," says the turkey.

"I will, then," says the little red hen. "Cluck! cluck!"

So she threshed the wheat.

"Who will take this wheat to mill to have it ground?" says the little red hen.

"I won't," says the dog.
"I won't," says the cat.
"I won't," says the pig.
"I won't," says the turkey.
"I will, then," says the little red hen. "Cluck! cluck!"

So she took the wheat to mill, and by and by she came back with the flour.

"Who will bake this flour?" says the little red hen.
"I won't," says the dog.
"I won't," says the cat.
"I won't," says the pig.
"I won't," says the turkey.
"I will, then," says the little red hen. "Cluck! cluck!"

So she baked the flour and made a loaf of bread.

"Who will eat this bread?" says the little red hen.
"I will," says the dog.
"I will," says the cat.
"I will," says the pig.
"I will," says the turkey.
"No, *I* will," says the little red hen. "Cluck! cluck!"

And she ate up the loaf of bread.

The King and His Hawk

RETOLD BY JAMES BALDWIN

Thomas Jefferson once advised us about how to control our temper: When angry, count to ten before you do anything, and when very angry, count to a hundred. Genghis Khan learned the same lesson eight hundred years ago. His empire stretched from eastern Europe to the Sea of Japan.

Genghis Khan was a great king and warrior.

He led his army into China and Persia, and he conquered many lands. In every country, men told about his daring deeds, and they said that since Alexander the Great there had been no king like him.

One morning when he was home from the wars, he rode out into the woods to have a day's sport. Many of his friends were with him. They rode out gaily, carrying their bows and arrows. Behind them came the servants with the hounds.

It was a merry hunting party. The woods rang with their shouts and laughter. They expected to carry much game home in the evening.

On the king's wrist sat his favorite hawk, for in those days hawks were trained to hunt. At a word from their masters they would fly high up into the air, and look around for prey. If they chanced to see a deer or a rabbit, they would swoop down upon it swift as any arrow.

All day long Genghis Khan and his huntsmen rode through the woods. But they did not find as much game as they expected.

Toward evening they started for home. The king had often ridden through the woods, and he knew all the paths. So while the rest of the party took the nearest way, he went by a longer road through a valley between two mountains.

The day had been warm, and the king was very thirsty. His pet hawk had left his wrist and flown away. It would be sure to find its way home.

The king rode slowly along. He had once seen a spring of clear water near this pathway. If he could only find it now! But the hot days of summer had dried up all the mountain brooks.

At last, to his joy, he saw some water trickling down over the edge of a rock. He knew that there was a spring farther up. In the wet season, a swift stream of water always poured down here, but now it came only one drop at a time.

The king leaped from his horse. He took a little silver cup from his hunting bag. He held it so as to catch the slowly falling drops.

It took a long time to fill the cup; the king was so thirsty that he could hardly wait. At last it was nearly full. He put the cup to his lips, and was about to drink.

All at once there was a whirring sound in the air, and the cup was knocked from his hands. The water was all spilled upon the ground.

The king looked up to see who had done this thing. It was his pet hawk.

The hawk flew back and forth a few times, and then alighted among the rocks by the spring.

The king picked up the cup, and again held it to catch the trickling drops.

This time he did not wait so long. When the cup was half full, he lifted it toward his mouth. But before it had touched his lips, the hawk swooped down again, and knocked it from his hands.

And now the king began to grow angry. He tried again, and for the third time the hawk kept him from drinking. The king was now very angry indeed.

"How do you dare to act so?" he cried. "If I had you in my hands, I would wring your neck!"

Then he filled the cup again. But before he tried to drink, he drew his sword.

"Now, Sir Hawk," he said, "this is the last time."

He had hardly spoken before the hawk swooped down and knocked the cup from his hand. But the king was looking for this. With a quick sweep of the sword he struck the bird as it passed.

The next moment the poor hawk lay bleeding and dying at its master's feet.

"That is what you get for your pains," said Genghis Khan.

But when he looked for his cup, he found that it had fallen between two rocks, where he could not reach it.

"At any rate, I will have a drink from that spring," he said to himself.

With that he began to climb the steep bank to the place from which the water trickled. It was hard work, and the higher he climbed, the thirstier he became.

At last he reached the place. There indeed was a pool of water; but what was that lying in the pool, and almost filling it? It was a huge, dead snake of the most poisonous kind.

The king stopped. He forgot his thirst. He thought only of the poor dead bird lying on the ground below him.

"The hawk saved my life!" he cried, "and how did I repay him? He was my best friend, and I have killed him."

He clambered down the bank. He took the bird up gently, and laid it in his hunting bag. Then he mounted his horse and rode swiftly home. He said to himself, "I have learned a sad lesson today, and that is, never to do anything in anger."

Hercules and the Wagoner

AESOP

This old fable helps us learn early that the only certain labor is our own.

A wagoner was driving his team along a muddy lane with a full load behind them, when the wheels of his wagon sank so deep in the mire that no efforts of his horses could move them. As he stood there, looking helplessly on, and calling loudly at intervals upon Hercules for assistance, the god himself appeared, and said to him, "Put your shoulder to the wheel, man, and goad on your horses, and then you may call on Hercules to assist you. If you won't lift a finger to help yourself, you can't expect Hercules or anyone else to come to your aid."

Heaven helps those who help themselves.

St. George and the Dragon

Retold by J. Berg Esenwein
and Marietta Stockard

"Somewhere perhaps there is trouble and fear," St. George says in this story before riding off to "find work which only a knight can do." Such people who go out of their way to help are sometimes called knights, saints; sometimes they are called ministers, teachers, and parents.

Long ago, when the knights lived in the land, there was one knight whose name was Sir George. He was not only braver than all the rest, but he was so noble, kind, and good that the people came to call him Saint George.

No robbers ever dared to trouble the people who lived near his castle, and all the wild animals were killed or driven away, so the little children could play even in the woods without being afraid.

One day St. George rode throughout the country. Everywhere he saw the men busy at their work in the fields, the women singing at work in their homes, and the little children shouting at their play.

"These people are all safe and happy. They need me no more," said St. George.

"But somewhere perhaps there is trouble and fear. There may be someplace where little children cannot play in safety, some woman may have been carried away from her home—perhaps there are even dragons left to be slain. Tomorrow I shall ride away and never stop until I find work which only a knight can do."

Early the next morning St. George put on his helmet and all his shining armor, and fastened his sword at his side. Then he mounted his great white horse and rode out from his castle gate. Down the steep, rough road he went, sitting straight and tall, and looking brave and strong as a knight should look.

On through the little village at the foot of the hill and

out across the country he rode. Everywhere he saw rich fields filled with waving grain, everywhere there was peace and plenty.

He rode on and on until at last he came into a part of the country he had never seen before. He noticed that there were no men working in the fields. The houses which he passed stood silent and empty. The grass along the roadside was scorched as if a fire had passed over it. A field of wheat was all trampled and burned.

St. George drew up his horse, and looked carefully about him. Everywhere there was silence and desolation. "What can be the dreadful thing that has driven all the people from their homes? I must find out, and give them help if I can," he said.

But there was no one to ask, so St. George rode forward until at last far in the distance he saw the walls of a city. "Here surely I shall find someone who can tell me the cause of all this," he said, so he rode more swiftly toward the city.

Just then the great gate opened and St. George saw crowds of people standing inside the wall. Some of them were weeping, all of them seemed afraid. As St. George watched, he saw a beautiful maiden dressed in white, with a girdle of scarlet about her waist, pass through the gate alone. The gate clanged shut and the maiden walked along the road, weeping bitterly. She did not see St. George, who was riding quickly toward her.

"Maiden, why do you weep?" he asked as he reached her side.

She looked up at St. George sitting there on his horse, straight and tall and beautiful. "Oh, Sir Knight!" she cried, "ride quickly from this place. You know not the danger you are in!"

"Danger!" said St. George. "Do you think a knight would flee from danger? Besides, you, a fair girl, are here alone. Think you a knight would leave you so? Tell me your trouble that I may help you."

"No! No!" she cried, "hasten away. You would only lose your life. There is a terrible dragon near. He may come at any moment. One breath would destroy you if he found you here. Go! Go quickly!"

"Tell me more of this," said St. George sternly. "Why are you here alone to meet this dragon? Are there no men left in yon city?"

"Oh," said the maiden, "my father, the King, is old and feeble. He has only me to help him take care of his people. This terrible dragon has driven them from their homes, carried away their cattle, and ruined their crops. They have all come within the walls of the city for safety. For weeks now the dragon has come to the very gates of the city. We have been forced to give him two sheep each day for his breakfast.

"Yesterday there were no sheep left to give, so he said that unless a young maiden were given him today he would break down the walls and destroy the city. The people cried to my father to save them, but he could do nothing. I am going to give myself to the dragon. Perhaps if he has me, the Princess, he may spare our people."

"Lead the way, brave Princess. Show me where this monster may be found."

When the Princess saw St. George's flashing eyes and great, strong arm as he drew forth his sword, she felt afraid no more. Turning, she led the way to a shining pool.

"There's where he stays," she whispered. "See, the water moves. He is waking."

St. George saw the head of the dragon lifted from the pool. Fold on fold he rose from the water. When he saw St. George he gave a roar of rage and plunged toward him. The smoke and flames flew from his nostrils, and he opened his great jaws as if to swallow both the knight and his horse.

St. George shouted and, waving his sword above his head, rode at the dragon. Quick and hard came the blows from St. George's sword. It was a terrible battle.

At last the dragon was wounded. He roared with pain and plunged at St. George, opening his great mouth close to the brave knight's head.

St. George looked carefully, then struck with all his strength straight down through the dragon's throat, and the dragon fell at the horse's feet—dead.

Then St. George shouted for joy at his victory. He called to the Princess. She came and stood beside him.

"Give me the girdle from about your waist, O Princess," said St. George.

The Princess gave him her girdle and St. George bound it around the dragon's neck, and they pulled the dragon after them by that little silken ribbon back to the city so that all of the people could see that the dragon could never harm them again.

When they saw St. George bringing the Princess back in safety and knew that the dragon was slain, they threw open the gates of the city and sent up great shouts of joy.

The King heard them and came out from his palace to see why the people were shouting.

When he saw his daughter safe he was the happiest of them all.

"O brave knight," he said, "I am old and weak. Stay here and help me guard my people from harm."

"I'll stay as long as ever you have need of me," St. George answered.

So he lived in the palace and helped the old King take care of his people, and when the old King died, St. George was made King in his stead. The people felt happy and safe so long as they had such a brave and good man for their King.

COMPASSION

FAITH

A Child's Prayer

Prayer, like all good habits, is best learned while we are very young.

Lord, teach a little child to pray,
And then accept my prayer;
For thou canst hear the words I say,
For thou art everywhere.

A little sparrow cannot fall
Unnoticed, Lord, by thee;
And though I am so young and small,
Thou dost take care of me.

Teach me to do the thing that's right,
And when I sin, forgive;
And make it still my chief delight
To serve thee while I live.

Kindness to Animals

Think of all creatures great and small.

Little children, never give
Pain to things that feel and live;
Let the gentle robin come
For the crumbs you save at home;
As his meat you throw along
He'll repay you with a song.
Never hurt the timid hare
Peeping from her green grass lair,
Let her come and sport and play
On the lawn at close of day.
The little lark goes soaring high
To the bright windows of the sky,
Singing as if 'twere always spring,
And fluttering on an untired wing—
Oh! let him sing his happy song,
Nor do these gentle creatures wrong.

The Sermon to the Birds

RETOLD BY JAMES BALDWIN

St. Francis was born 800 years ago in Italy. He is still admired for his simple life of poverty, his love of peace, and his respect for all living things.

Very kind and loving was St. Francis—kind and loving not only to men but to all living things. He spoke of the birds as his little brothers of the air, and he could never bear to see them harmed.

At Christmastime he scattered crumbs of bread under the trees, so that the tiny creatures could feast and be happy.

Once when a boy gave him a pair of doves which he had snared, St. Francis had a nest made for them, and the mother bird laid her eggs in it.

By and by, the eggs hatched, and a nestful of young doves grew up. They were so tame that they sat on the shoulders of St. Francis and ate from his hand.

And many other stories are told of this man's great love and pity for the timid creatures which lived in the fields and woods.

One day as he was walking among the trees the birds saw him and flew down to greet him. They sang their sweetest songs to show how much they loved him. Then, when they saw that he was about to speak, they nestled softly in the grass and listened.

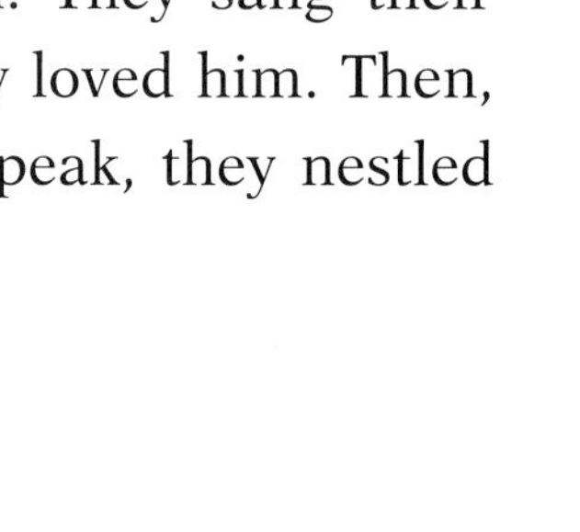

"O little birds," he said, "I love you, for you are my brothers and sisters of the air. Let me tell you something, my little brothers, my little sisters: You ought always to love God and praise Him.

"For think what He has given you. He has given you wings with which to fly through the air. He has given you clothing both warm and beautiful. He has given you the air in which to move and have homes.

"And think of this, O little brothers: you sow not, neither do you reap, for God feeds you. He gives you the rivers and the brooks from which to drink. He gives you the mountains and the valleys where you may rest. He gives you the trees in which to build your nests.

"You toil not, neither do you spin, yet God takes care of you and your little ones. It must be, then, that He loves you. So, do not be ungrateful, but sing His praises and thank Him for his goodness toward you."

Then the saint stopped speaking and looked around him. All the birds sprang up joyfully. They spread their wings and opened their mouths to show that they understood his words.

And when he had blessed them, all began to sing; and the whole forest was filled with sweetness and joy because of their wonderful melodies.

Someone Sees You

Faith tells us that no act goes unseen. We are likely to act better with such faith.

Once upon a time a man decided to sneak into his neighbor's fields and steal some wheat. "If I take just a little from each field, no one will notice," he told himself, "but it will all add up to a nice pile of wheat for me." So he waited for the darkest night, when thick clouds lay over the moon, and he crept out of his house. He took his youngest daughter with him.

"Daughter," he whispered, "you must stand guard, and call out if anyone sees me."

The man stole into the first field to begin reaping, and before long the child called out, "Father, someone sees you!"

The man looked all around, but he saw no one, so he gathered his stolen wheat and moved on to a second field.

"Father, someone sees you!" the child cried again.

The man stopped and looked all around, but once again he saw no one. He gathered more wheat, and moved to a third field.

A little while passed, and the daughter cried out, "Father, someone sees you!"

Once more the man stopped his work and looked in every direction, but he saw no one at all, so he bundled his wheat and crept into the last field.

"Father, someone sees you!" the child called again.

The man stopped his reaping, looked all around, and once again saw no one. "Why in the world do you keep saying someone sees me?" he angrily asked his daughter. "I've looked everywhere, and I don't see anyone."

"Father," murmured the child, "Someone sees you from above."

The Honest Disciple

As this Jewish folktale reminds us, faith is often the path to other virtues (in this case, honesty).

Once a rabbi decided to test the honesty of his disciples, so he called them together and posed a question.

"What would you do if you were walking along and found a purse full of money lying in the road?" he asked.

"I'd return it to its owner," said one disciple.

"His answer comes so quickly, I must wonder if he really means it," the rabbi thought.

"I'd keep the money if nobody saw me find it," said another.

"He has a frank tongue, but a wicked heart," the rabbi told himself.

"Well, Rabbi," said a third disciple, "to be honest, I believe I'd be tempted to keep it. So I would pray to God that He give me the strength to resist such temptation and do the right thing."

"Aha!" thought the rabbi. "Here is the man I would trust."

Little Sunshine

RETOLD BY ETTA AUSTIN BLAISDELL AND MARY FRANCES BLAISDELL

Bestowing compassion is like offering most other gifts. Often it's the thought that counts.

Once there was a little girl named Elsa. She had a very old grandmother, with white hair, and wrinkles all over her face.

Elsa's father had a large house that stood on a hill.

Each day the sun peeped in at the south windows. It made everything look bright and beautiful.

The grandmother lived on the north side of the house. The sun never came to her room.

One day Elsa said to her father, "Why doesn't the sun peep into Grandma's room? I know she would like to have him."

"The sun cannot look in at the north windows," said her father.

"Then let us turn the house around, Papa."

"It is much too large for that," said her father.

"Will Grandma never have any sunshine in her room?" asked Elsa.

"Of course not, my child, unless you can carry some to her."

After that Elsa tried and tried to think how she could carry the sunshine to her grandmother.

When she played in the fields she saw the grass and the flowers nodding their heads. The birds sang sweetly as they flew from tree to tree.

Everything seemed to say, "We love the sun. We love the bright, warm sun."

"Grandma would love it, too," thought the child. "I must take some to her."

When she was in the garden one morning she felt the sun's warm rays in her golden hair. Then she sat down and she saw them in her lap.

"I will take them in my dress," she thought, "and carry them to Grandma's room." So she jumped up and ran into the house.

"Look, Grandma, Look! I have some sunshine for you," she cried. And she opened her dress, but there was not a ray to be seen.

"It peeps out of your eyes, my child," said her grandmother, "and it shines in your sunny, golden hair. I do not need the sun when I have you with me."

Elsa did not understand how the sun could peep out of her eyes. But she was glad to make her dear grandmother happy.

Every morning she played in the garden. Then she ran to her grandmother's room to carry the sunshine in her eyes and hair.

The Lion and the Mouse

AESOP

With kindness, the smallest can often help the biggest.

One day a great lion lay asleep in the sunshine. A little mouse ran across his paw and wakened him. The great lion was just going to eat him up when the little mouse cried, "Oh, please, let me go, sir. Some day I may help you."

The lion laughed at the thought that the little mouse could be of any use to him. But he was a good-natured lion, and he set the mouse free.

Not long after, the lion was caught in a net. He tugged and pulled with all his might, but the ropes were too strong. Then he roared loudly. The little mouse heard him, and ran to the spot.

"Be still, dear Lion, and I will set you free. I will gnaw the ropes."

With his sharp little teeth, the mouse cut the ropes, and the lion came out of the net.

"You laughed at me once," said the mouse. "You thought I was too little to do you a good turn. But see, you owe your life to a poor little mouse."

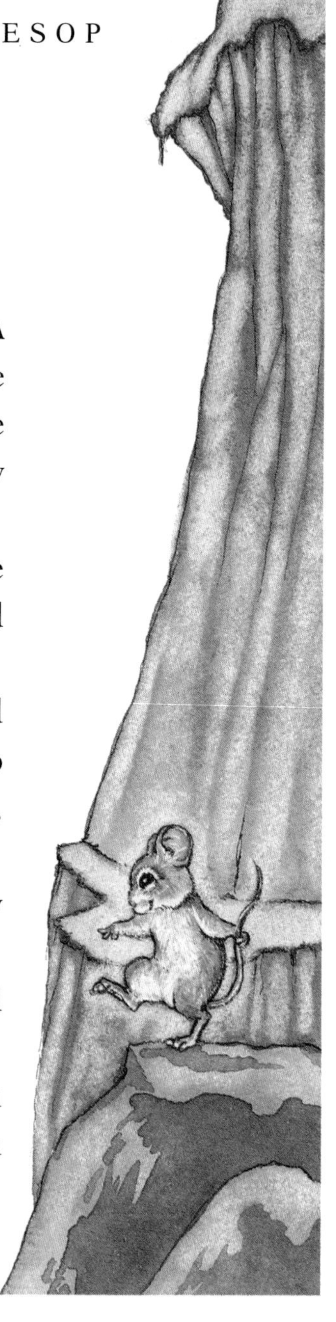

The Legend of the Dipper

RETOLD BY J. BERG ESENWEIN AND MARIETTA STOCKARD

A kind act is often its own reward.

There had been no rain in the land for a very long time. It was so hot and dry that the flowers were withered, the grass was parched and brown, and even the big, strong trees were dying. The water dried up in the creeks and rivers, the wells were dry, the fountains stopped bubbling. The cows, the dogs, the horses, the birds, and all the people were so thirsty! Everyone felt uncomfortable and sick.

There was one little girl whose mother grew very ill. "Oh," said the little girl, "if I can only find some water for my mother I'm sure she will be well again. I must find some water."

So she took a tin cup and started out in search of water. By and by she found a tiny little spring away up on a mountainside. It was almost dry. The water dropped, dropped, ever so slowly from under the rock. The little girl held her cup carefully and caught the drops. She waited and waited a long, long time until the cup was full of water. Then she started down the mountain holding the cup very carefully, for she didn't want to spill a single drop.

On the way she passed a poor little dog. He could hardly drag himself along. He was panting for breath and his tongue hung from his mouth because it was so dry and parched.

"Oh, you poor little dog," said the little girl, "you are so thirsty. I can't pass you without giving you a few drops of water. If I give you just a little there will still be enough for my mother."

So the little girl poured some water into her hand and held it down for the little dog. He lapped it up quickly and then he felt so much better that he frisked and barked and seemed almost to say, "Thank you, little girl." And the little girl didn't notice—but her tin dipper had changed into a silver dipper and was just as full of water as it had been before.

She thought about her mother and hurried along as fast as she could go. When she reached home it was late in the afternoon, almost dark. The little girl pushed the door open and hurried up to her mother's room. When she came into the room the old servant who helped the little girl and her mother, and had been working hard all day taking care of the sick woman, came to the door. She was so tired and so thirsty that she couldn't even speak to the little girl.

"Do give her some water," said the mother. "She has worked hard all day and she needs it much more than I do."

So the little girl held the cup to her lips and the old servant drank some of the water. She felt stronger and better right away and she went over to the mother and lifted her up. The little girl didn't notice that the cup had changed into a gold cup and was just as full of water as it was before!

Then she held the cup to her mother's lips and she drank and drank. Oh, she felt so much better! When she had finished there was still some water left in the cup. The little girl was just raising it to her own lips when there came a knock at the door. The servant opened it and there stood a stranger. He was very pale and all covered with dust from traveling. "I am thirsty," he said. "Won't you give me a little water?"

The little girl said, "Why, certainly I will, I am sure that you need it far more than I do. Drink it all."

The stranger smiled and took the dipper in his hand, and as he took it, it changed into a diamond dipper. He turned it upside down and all the water spilled out and sank into the ground. And where it spilled a fountain bubbled up. The cool water flowed and splashed—enough for the people and all the animals in the whole land to have all the water they wanted to drink.

As they watched the water they forgot the stranger, but presently when they looked he was gone. They thought they could see him just vanishing in the sky—and there in the sky, clear and high, shone the diamond dipper. It shines up there yet, and reminds people of the little girl who was kind and unselfish. It is called the Big Dipper.

HONESTY • LOYALTY • FRIENDSHIP

The Pasture

ROBERT FROST

This little poem reminds us that a friend is someone we want to be with.

I'm going out to clean the pasture spring;
I'll only stop to rake the leaves away
(And wait to watch the water clear, I may):
I sha'n't be gone long.—You come too.

I'm going out to fetch the little calf
That's standing by the mother. It's so young,
It totters when she licks it with her tongue.
I sha'n't be long.—You come too.

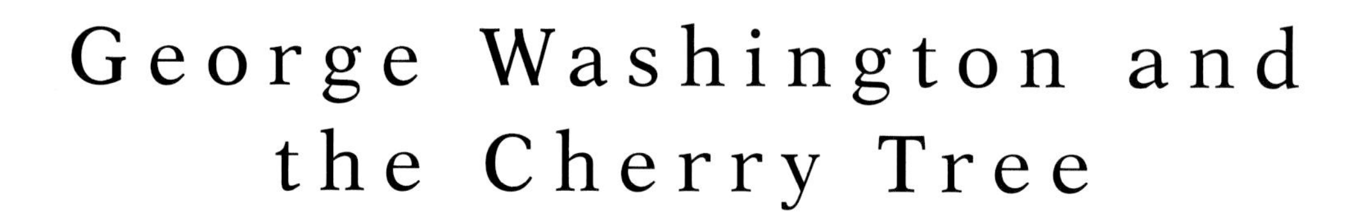

George Washington and the Cherry Tree

Adapted from J. Berg Esenwein and Marietta Stockard

Here is the most famous American story about telling the truth. We should all be like young George.

When George Washington was a little boy he lived on a farm in Virginia. His father taught him to ride, and he used to take young George about the farm with him so that his son might learn how to take care of the fields and horses and cattle when he grew older.

Mr. Washington had planted an orchard of fine fruit trees. There were apple trees, peach trees, pear trees, plum trees, and cherry trees. Once, a particularly fine cherry tree was sent to him from across the ocean. Mr. Washington planted it on the edge of the orchard. He told everyone on the farm to watch it carefully to see that it was not broken or hurt in any way.

It grew well and one spring it was covered with white blossoms. Mr. Washington was pleased to think he would soon have cherries from the little tree.

Just about this time, George was given a shiny new hatchet. George took it and went about chopping sticks, hacking into the rails of fences, and cutting whatever else he passed. At last he came to the edge of the orchard, and thinking only of how well his hatchet could cut, he chopped into the little cherry tree. The bark was soft, and it cut so easily that George chopped the tree right down, and then went on with his play.

That evening when Mr. Washington came from inspecting the farm, he sent his horse to the stable and walked down to the orchard to look at his cherry tree. He stood in amazement when he saw how it was cut. Who would have dared do such a thing? He asked everyone, but no one could tell him anything about it.

Just then George passed by.

"George," his father called in an angry voice, "do you know who killed my cherry tree?"

This was a tough question, and George staggered under it for a moment, but quickly recovered.

"I cannot tell a lie, father," he said. "I did it with my hatchet."

Mr. Washington looked at George. The boy's face was white, but he looked straight into his father's eyes.

"Go into the house, son," said Mr. Washington sternly.

George went into the library and waited for his father. He was very unhappy and very much ashamed. He knew he had been foolish and thoughtless and that his father was right to be displeased.

Soon, Mr. Washington came into the room. "Come here, my boy," he said.

George went over to his father. Mr. Washington looked at him long and steadily.

"Tell me, son, why did you cut the tree?"

"I was playing and I did not think—" George stammered.

"And now the tree will die. We shall never have any cherries from it. But worse than that, you have failed to take care of the tree when I asked you to do so."

George's head was bent and his cheeks were red from shame.

"I am sorry, father," he said.

Mr. Washington put his hand on the boy's shoulder. "Look at me," he said. "I am sorry to have lost my cherry tree, but I am glad that you were brave enough to tell me the truth. I would rather have you truthful and brave than to have a whole orchard full of the finest cherry trees. Never forget that, my son."

George Washington never did forget. To the end of his life he was just as brave and honorable as he was that day as a little boy.

God Make My Life a Little Light

M. BENTHAM-EDWARDSTHAT

Friends give of themselves.

God make my life a little light,
Within the world to glow;
A tiny flame that burneth bright
Wherever I may go.

God make my life a little flower,
That giveth joy to all,
Content to bloom in native bower,
Although its place be small.

God make my life a little staff,
Whereon the weak may rest,
That so what health and strength I have
May serve my neighbors best.

The Indian Cinderella

RETOLD BY CYRUS MACMILLAN

This Native American tale from Canada is about how honesty is rewarded and dishonesty punished. Glooskap, mentioned in the opening paragraph, was a god of the Eastern woodlands Indians.

On the shores of a wide bay on the Atlantic coast there dwelt in old times a great Indian warrior. It was said that he had been one of Glooskap's best helpers and friends, and that he had done for him many wonderful deeds. But that, no man knows. He had, however, a very wonderful and strange power: he could make himself invisible. He could thus mingle unseen with his enemies and listen to their plots. He was known among the people as Strong Wind, the Invisible. He dwelt with his sister in a tent near the sea, and his sister helped him greatly in his work. Many maidens would have been glad to marry him, and he was much sought after because of his mighty deeds; and it was known that Strong Wind would marry the first maiden who could see him as he came home at night. Many made the trial, but it was a long time before one succeeded. Strong Wind used a clever trick to test the truthfulness of all who sought to win him.

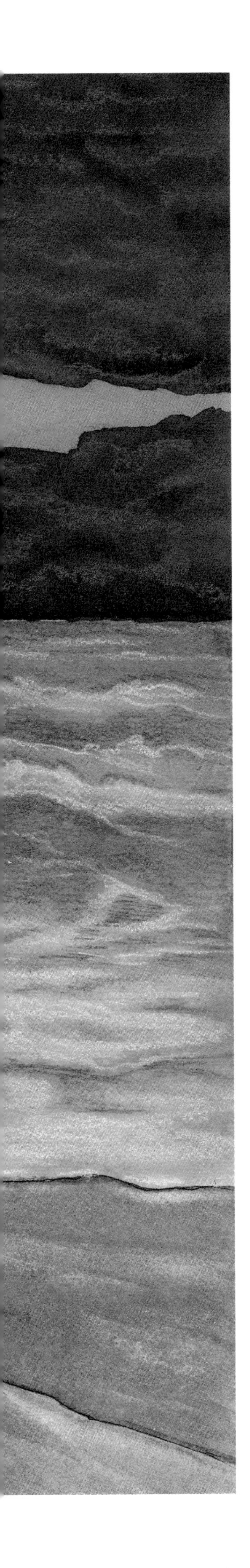

Each evening as the day went down, his sister walked on the beach with any girl who wished to make the trial. His sister could always see him, but no one else could see him. And as he came home from work in the twilight, his sister, as she saw him drawing near, would ask the girl who sought him, "Do you see him?" And each girl would falsely answer "Yes." And his sister would ask, "With what does he draw his sled?" And each girl would answer, "With the hide of a moose," or "With a pole," or "With a great cord." And then his sister would know that they all had lied, for their answers were mere guesses. And many tried and lied and failed, for Strong Wind would not marry any who were untruthful.

There lived in the village a great chief who had three daughters. Their mother had long been dead. One of these was much younger than the others. She was very beautiful and gentle and well beloved by all, and for that reason her older sisters were very jealous of her charms and treated her very cruelly. They clothed her in rags that she might be ugly; and they cut off her long black hair; and they burned her face with coals from the fire that she might be scarred and disfigured. And they lied to their father, telling him that she had done these things herself. But the girl was patient and kept her gentle heart and went gladly about her work.

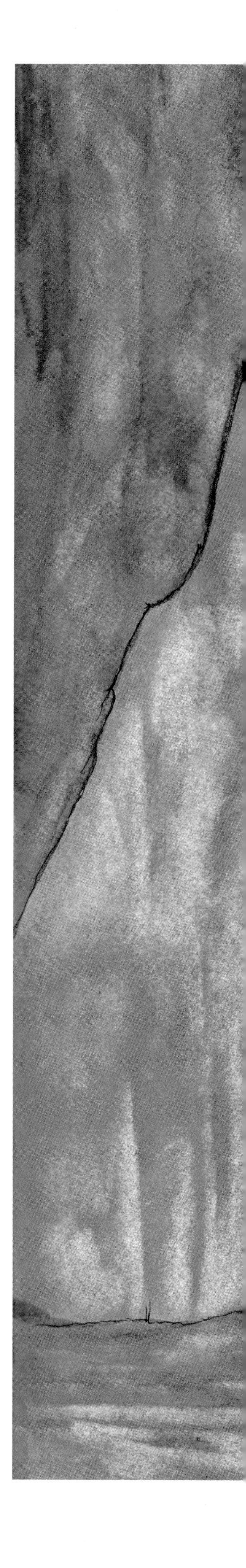

Like other girls, the chief's two eldest daughters tried to win Strong Wind. One evening, as the day went down, they walked on the shore with Strong Wind's sister and waited for his coming. Soon he came home from his day's work, drawing his sled. And his sister asked as usual, "Do you see him?" And each one, lying, answered "Yes." And she asked, "Of what is his shoulder strap made?" And each, guessing, said "Of rawhide." Then they entered the tent where they hoped to see Strong Wind eating his supper; and when he took off his coat and his moccasins they could see them, but more than these they saw nothing. And Strong Wind knew that they had lied, and he kept himself from their sight, and they went home dismayed.

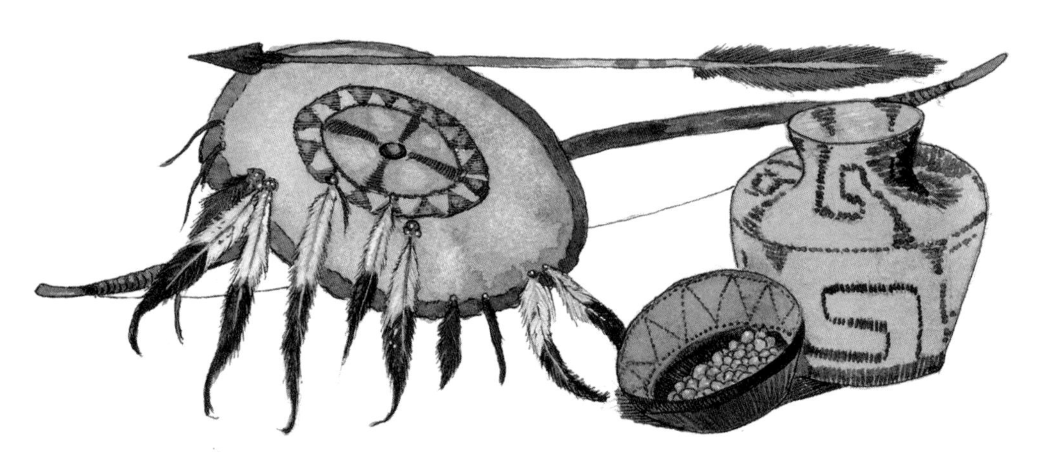

One day the chief's youngest daughter with her rags and burned face resolved to seek Strong Wind. She patched her clothes with bits of birch bark from the trees, and put on the few little ornaments she possessed, and went forth to try to see the Invisible One as all the other girls of the village had done before. And her sisters laughed at her and called her "fool." And as she passed along the road all the people laughed at her because of her tattered frock and her burned face, but silently she went her way.

Strong Wind's sister received the girl kindly, and at twilight she took her to the beach. Soon Strong Wind came home drawing his sled. And his sister asked, "Do you see him?" And the girl answered "No," and his sister wondered greatly because she spoke the truth. And again she asked, "Do you see him now?" And the girl answered, "Yes, and he is very wonderful." And she asked, "With what does he draw his sled?" And the girl answered, "With the Rainbow," and she was much afraid. And she asked further, "Of what is his bowstring?" And the girl answered, "His bowstring is the Milky Way."

Then Strong Wind's sister knew that because the girl had spoken the truth at first her brother had made himself visible to her. And she said, "Truly, you have seen him." And she took the girl home and bathed her, and all the scars disappeared from her face and body; and her hair grew long and black again like the raven's wing; and she gave her fine clothes to wear and many rich ornaments. Then she bade her take the wife's seat in the tent. Soon Strong Wind entered and sat beside her, and called her his bride.

The very next day she became his wife, and ever afterward she helped him to do great deeds. The girl's two elder sisters were very cross and they wondered greatly at what had taken place. But Strong Wind, who knew of their cruelty, resolved to punish them. Using his great power, he changed them both into aspen trees and rooted them in the earth. And since that day the leaves of the aspen have always trembled, and they shiver in fear at the approach of Strong Wind; it matters not how softly he comes, for they are still mindful of his great power and anger because of their lies and their cruelty to their sister long ago.

Little Boy Blue

EUGENE FIELD

Some of our earliest, most faithful friends are our childhood toys. May we all learn to be as steadfast in our loyalties as the companions of Little Boy Blue.

The little toy dog is covered with dust,
  But sturdy and stanch he stands;
And the little toy soldier is red with rust,
  And his musket molds in his hands.
Time was when the little toy dog was new
  And the soldier was passing fair;
And that was the time when our Little Boy Blue
  Kissed them and put them there.

"Now, don't you go till I come," he said,
  "And don't you make any noise!"
So, toddling off to his trundle-bed,
  He dreamed of the pretty toys;
And as he was dreaming, an angel song
  Awakened our Little Boy Blue—
Oh! the years are many, the years are long,
  But the little toy friends are true!

Aye, faithful to Little Boy Blue they stand,
  Each in the same old place—
Awaiting the touch of a little hand,
  And the smile of a little face;
And they wonder, as waiting these long years through
  In the dust of that little chair,
What has become of our Little Boy Blue,
  Since he kissed them and put them there.

The Boy Who Cried "Wolf"

AESOP

The fastest way to lose what we call our good character is to lose our honesty.

There was once a shepherd boy who kept his flock at a little distance from the village. Once he thought he would play a trick on the villagers and have some fun at their expense. So he ran toward the village crying out, with all his might: "Wolf! Wolf! Come and help! The wolves are at my lambs!"

The kind villagers left their work and ran to the field to help him. But when they got there the boy laughed at them for their pains; there was no wolf there.

Still another day the boy tried the same trick, and the villagers came running to help and were laughed at again.

Then one day a wolf did break into the fold and began killing the lambs. In great fright, the boy ran back for help. "Wolf! Wolf!" he screamed. "There is a wolf in the flock! Help!"

The villagers heard him, but they thought it was another mean trick; no one paid the least attention, or went near him. And the shepherd boy lost all his sheep.

That is the kind of thing that happens to people who lie: even when they do tell the truth they will not be believed.

The Honest Woodman

Adapted from Emilie Poulsson

This old fable, told around the world, shows us that honesty pays.

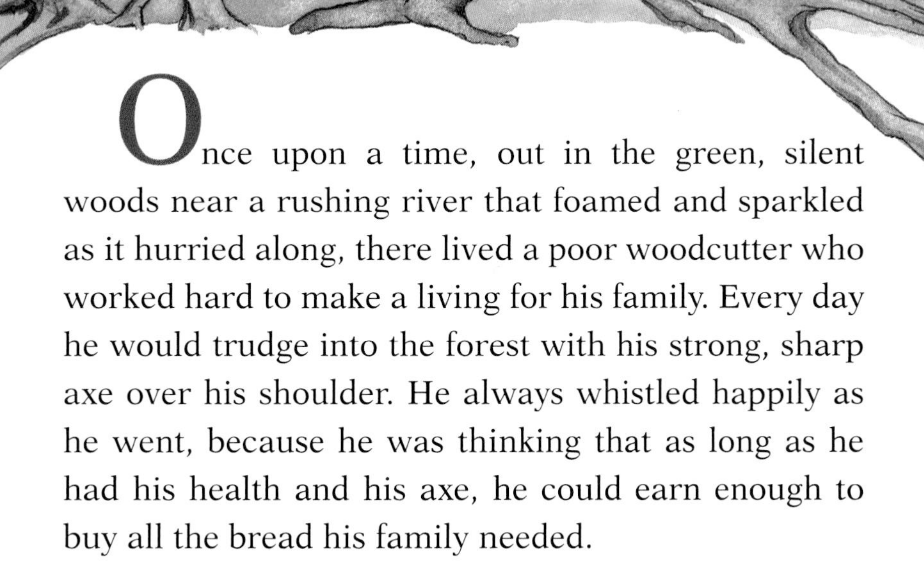

Once upon a time, out in the green, silent woods near a rushing river that foamed and sparkled as it hurried along, there lived a poor woodcutter who worked hard to make a living for his family. Every day he would trudge into the forest with his strong, sharp axe over his shoulder. He always whistled happily as he went, because he was thinking that as long as he had his health and his axe, he could earn enough to buy all the bread his family needed.

One day he was cutting a large oak tree near the riverside. The chips flew fast at every stroke, and the sound of the ringing axe echoed through the forest so clearly you might have thought a dozen wood choppers were at work that day.

By and by the woodman thought he would rest awhile. He leaned his axe against the tree and turned to sit down, but he tripped over an old, gnarled root, and before he could catch it, his axe slid down the bank and into the river!

The poor woodman gazed into the stream, trying to see the bottom, but it was far too deep there. The river flowed over the lost treasure just as merrily as before.

"What will I do?" the woodman cried. "I've lost my axe! How will I feed my children now?"

Just as he finished speaking, up from the lake rose a beautiful lady. She was the water fairy of the river, and came to the surface when she heard his sad voice.

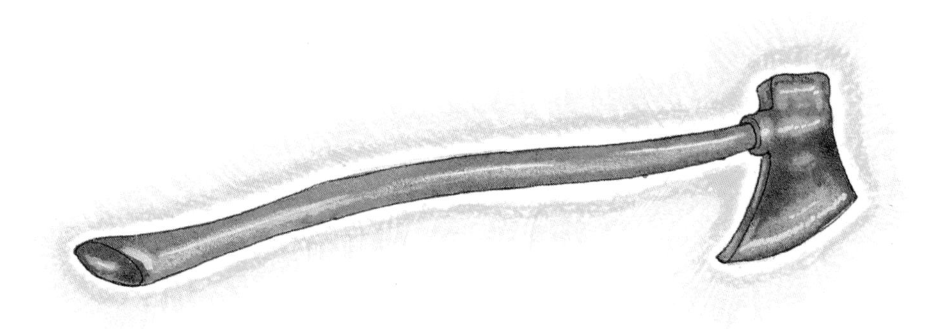

"What is your sorrow?" she asked kindly. The woodman told her about his trouble, and at once she sank beneath the surface, and reappeared in a moment with an axe made of silver.

"Is this the axe you lost?" she asked.

The woodman thought of all the fine things he could buy for his children with that silver! But the axe wasn't his, so he shook his head, and answered, "My axe was only made of steel."

The water fairy lay the silver axe on the bank, and sank into the river again. In a moment she rose and showed the woodman another axe. "Perhaps this one is yours?" she asked.

The woodman looked. "Oh, no!" he replied. "This one is made of gold! It's worth many times more than mine."

The water fairy lay the golden axe on the bank. Once again she sank. Up she rose. This time she held the missing axe.

"That is mine!" The woodman cried. "That is surely my old axe!"

"It is yours," said the water fairy, "and so are these other two now. They are gifts from the river, because you have told the truth."

And that evening the woodman trudged home with all three axes on his shoulder, whistling happily as he thought of all the good things they would bring for his family.

Why Frog and Snake Never Play Together

This African folktale makes us think about how much companionship the world has missed because people are told they "can't" be friends with each other.

Once upon a time, the child of the Frog was hopping along in the bush when he spied someone new lying across the path before him. This someone was long and slender, and his skin seemed to shine with all the colors of the rainbow.

"Hello there," called Frog-child. "What are you doing lying here in the path?"

"Just warming myself in the sun," answered the someone new, twisting and turning and uncoiling himself. "My name is Snake-child. What's yours?"

"I'm Frog-child. Would you like to play with me?"

So Frog-child and Snake-child played together all morning long in the bush.

"Watch what I can do," said Frog-child, and he hopped high into the air. "I'll teach you how, if you want," he offered.

So he taught Snake-child how to hop, and together they hopped up and down the path through the bush.

"Now watch what I can do," said Snake-child, and he crawled on his belly straight up the trunk of a tall tree. "I'll teach you if you want."

So he taught Frog-child how to slide on his belly and climb into trees.

After a while they both grew hungry and decided to go home for lunch, but they promised each other to meet again the next day.

"Thanks for teaching me how to hop," called Snake-child.

"Thanks for teaching me how to crawl up trees," called Frog-child.

Then they each went home.

"Look what I can do, Mother!" cried Frog-child, crawling on his belly.

"Where did you learn how to do that?" his mother asked.

"Snake-child taught me," he answered. "We played together in the bush this morning. He's my new friend."

"Don't you know the Snake family is a bad family?" his mother asked. "They have poison in their teeth. Don't ever let me catch you playing with one of them again. And don't let me see you crawling on your belly, either. It isn't proper."

Meanwhile, Snake-child went home and hopped up and down for his mother to see

"Who taught you to do that?" she asked.

"Frog-child did," he said. "He's my new friend.'

"What foolishness," said his mother. "Don't you know we've been on bad terms with the Frog family for longer than anyone can remember? The next time you play with Frog-child, catch him and eat him up. And stop that hopping. It isn't our custom."

So the next morning when Frog-child met Snake-child in the bush, he kept his distance

"I'm afraid I can't go crawling with you today," he called, hopping back a hop or two.

Snake-child eyed him quietly, remembering what his mother had told him. "If he gets too close, I'll spring at him and eat him," he thought. But then he remembered how much fun they had had together, and how nice Frog-child had been to teach him how to hop. So he sighed sadly to himself and slid away into the bush.

And from that day onward, Frog-child and Snake-child never played together again. But they often sat alone in the sun, each thinking about their one day of friendship.

THE CHILDREN'S Book of Heroes

EDITED BY

William J. Bennett

ILLUSTRATED BY

Michael Hague

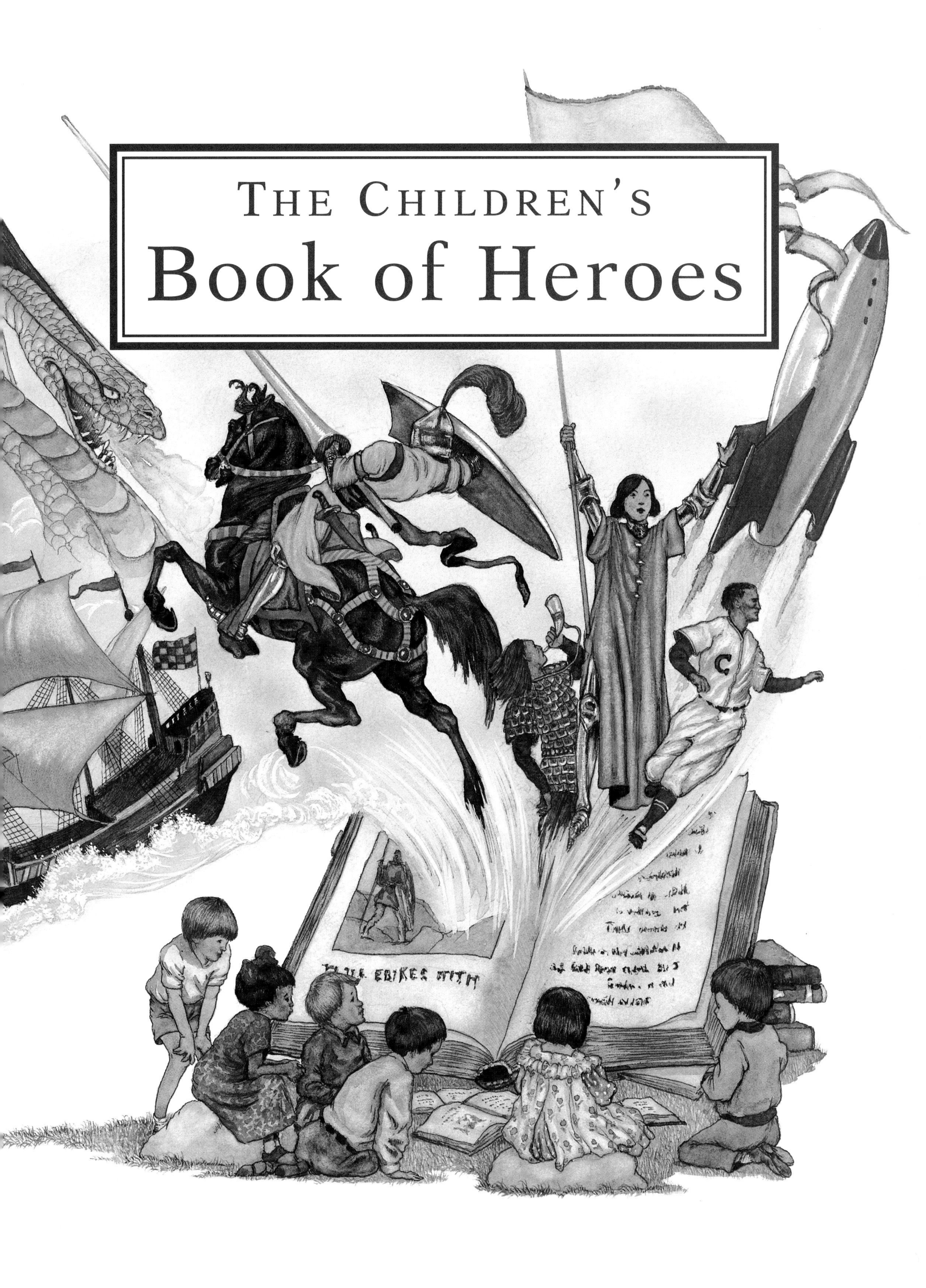
THE CHILDREN'S
Book of Heroes

CONTENTS

My wife, Elayne, helps me with many things, and she helped me with this book. Through her efforts it is a better and more beautiful book—just one of the reasons she is a hero to me, and to John and Joseph.
—W.J.B.

To Minnie Minoso
—M.H.

INTRODUCTION

When I was a boy, adults I knew went to the trouble of helping me find a few heroes. At first, the ones I admired most were not people I knew personally, but figures who nonetheless possessed qualities of human excellence worth striving for: baseball and football players who persevered on and off the field, famous explorers from the pages of history who dared to face the unknown, cowboys from Hollywood Westerns who rode hard and stood up for what deserved to be loved and protected. As I grew older, I learned that heroes could be found closer to home, too—neighbors, friends, and members of my own family. In all of them, there was a certain nobility, a largeness of soul, a hitching up of one's own purposes to higher purposes—to something that demanded endurance or sacrifice or courage or compassion.

Looking back, I see how lucky I was that so many of my teachers thought it was worth their time to help me pick the right kind of heroes. As every parent knows, children imitate what they see and hear. They naturally look for examples to follow. Today's popular culture offers plenty. Countless "stars" and "superstars" are put on pedestals for children to idolize and mimic. The problem is that most are celebrities, not heroes (it has been said that the difference between the two is that while the hero is known for worthy actions, the celebrity is known for being well known). And often, especially in our times, the behaviors for which many celebrities are famous are not worthy of imitation. But little children don't know that. They can't foresee that some pedestals, in time, turn out to be shaky and come crashing down. So it makes a big difference whether or not adults make efforts to point out what actions merit honor and which individuals deserve to be admired.

This book is meant to aid parents in such efforts. Its heroes give young people targets to aim for and examples to follow. Their tales come to life in Michael Hague's charming, magical paintings, which speak to the hearts

and imaginations of children. The combination of a few good stories, Michael's illustrations, and a parent's voice reading aloud is a great way to lift children's thoughts toward what is noble and fine.

Some of these heroes are doers of ancient, famous deeds ("mighty men which were of old, men of renown," as the book of Genesis has it)—shining victors, knights in armor, adventurers on the high seas. Their stories often unfold in far-off places—dusty plains, stormy seas, dungeons dark, castles high. Theirs are tales of epic drama—battles against overwhelming odds, daring rescues, struggles to the death, triumphs of good over evil.

But in truth, most heroes are not men and women of great renown. They live close by and, more often than not, perform deeds noticed by only a few. You'll find those kinds of heroes here, too. They come from every walk of life—boys and girls, mothers and fathers, men and women of God, teachers, a neighbor lending a helping hand, the cop around the corner. They win our admiration by committing the sort of acts every one of us might be called upon to perform—by offering some unseen gesture of compassion, by taking a quiet stand for what is right, by managing to hang on just one minute longer, or perhaps by persevering through a lifetime of struggle and toil.

Some of the heroes in this book are real people. They have lived and breathed, just as you and I. Others tread only the worlds of our imaginations. But factual or fictional, they all put a face on and give a meaning to heroism. They give us a chance to say to children, "Look, there is a person who has done something worth imitating."

It is important to say that to children, because believing in the heroic can help make each and every one of us a little bit better, day in and day out. If our children are to reach for the best, they need to have a picture of the best.

I hope this book helps boys and girls to believe in heroes. I hope it inspires parents and children to look around them and together pick out a few heroes of their own.

Heroes

WILLIAM CANTON

Our favorite heroes live forever in their stories and in our memories, cheering us forward in our own brave fights.

For you who love heroic things
In summer dream or winter tale,
I tell of warriors, saints, and kings,
In scarlet, sackcloth, glittering mail,
And helmets peaked with iron wings.

They beat down Wrong; they strove for Right.
In ringing fields, on grappled ships,
Singing, they flung into the fight.
They fell with triumph on their lips,
And in their eyes a glorious light.

That light still gleams. From far away
Their brave song greets us like a cheer.
We fight the same great fight as they,
Right against Wrong; we, now and here;
They, in their fashion, yesterday.

Opportunity

~ Edward Rowland Sill

It's not the sword you use that makes you a hero. It's how you use the sword.

This I beheld, or dreamed it in a dream:
There spread a cloud of dust along a plain;
And underneath the cloud, or in it, raged
A furious battle, and men yelled, and swords
Shocked upon swords and shields. A prince's banner
Wavered, then staggered backward, hemmed by foes.
A craven hung along the battle's edge,
And thought: "Had I a sword of keener steel—
That blue blade that the king's son bears—but this
Blunt thing—!" he snapt and flung it from his hand,
And lowering crept away and left the field.
Then came the king's son, wounded, sore bestead,
And weaponless, and saw the broken sword,
Hilt buried in the dry and trodden sand,
And ran and snatched it, and with battle shout
Lifted afresh, he hewed his enemy down,
And saved a great cause that heroic day.

About Angels

—ADAPTED FROM LAURA E. RICHARDS

Here is a story about a guardian angel who is always close at hand, the kind who watches over you from the moment you come into the world.

"Mother," said the child, "are there really angels?"

"The Bible says so," said the mother.

"Yes," said the child. "I have seen the picture. But did you ever see one, Mother?"

"I think I have," said the mother, "but she was not dressed like the picture."

"I am going to find one!" said the child. "I am going to run along the road, miles and miles and miles, until I find an angel."

"That is a good plan!" said the mother. "And I will go with you, for you are too little to run far alone."

"I am not little anymore!" said the child. "I can tie my own shoes. I am big."

"So you are!" said the mother. "I forgot. But it is a fine day, and I should like the walk."

"But you walk so slowly, with your hurt foot."

"I can walk faster than you think!" said the mother.

So they started, the child leaping and running, and the mother stepping out so bravely with her injured foot that the child soon forgot about it.

The child danced ahead, and soon he saw a long, silver car coming toward him. In the back sat a splendidly dressed lady. As she moved in her seat, she flashed with jewels and gold, and her eyes were brighter than her diamonds.

The car rolled to a halt at a stop sign.

"Are you an angel?" asked the child, running up beside it.

The lady made no reply, but stared coldly at the child. Then she spoke a word to her driver, and the engine roared. The car sped away in a cloud of dust and fumes, and disappeared.

The dust filled the child's eyes and mouth, and made him choke and sneeze. He gasped for breath and rubbed his eyes, but presently his mother came up and wiped away the dust with the corner of her dress.

"That was not an angel!" said the child.

"No, indeed!" said the mother. "Nothing like one!"

The child danced on again, leaping and running from side to side of the road, and the mother followed as best she could.

By and by the child met a most beautiful young woman, clad in a white dress. Her eyes were like blue stars, and the blushes came and went in her face like roses looking through snow.

"I am sure you must be an angel!" cried the child.

The young woman blushed more sweetly than before. "You dear little child!" she cried. "Someone else said that only last evening. Do I really look like an angel?"

"You *are* an angel!" said the child.

The young woman took him up in her arms, and kissed him, and held him tenderly. "You are the dearest little thing I ever saw!" she said. "Tell me what makes you think so!" But suddenly her face changed.

"Oh!" she cried. "There he is, coming to meet me! And you have soiled my white dress with your dusty shoes, and messed up my beautiful hair. Run away, child, and go home to your mother!"

She set the child down, not unkindly, but so hastily that he stumbled and fell. But she did not see that, for she was hastening to meet her boyfriend, who was coming along the road. (Now if the young woman had only known, he thought her twice as lovely with the child in her arms, but she did not know.)

The child lay in the dusty road and sobbed, till his mother came along, picked him up, and wiped away the tears.

"I don't believe that was an angel, after all," he said.

"No!" said the mother. "But she may be one someday. She is young yet."

"I am tired!" said the child. "Will you carry me home, Mother?"

"Why, yes!" said the mother. "That is what I came for."

The child put his arms around his mother's neck, and she held him tight and trudged along the road, singing the song he liked best. Suddenly he looked up into her face.

"Mother," he said, "I don't suppose *you* could be an angel, could you?"

"Oh, my little one!" said the mother. "I am just your mother who loves you." And she went on singing, and stepped out so happily on her injured foot that she forgot her pain and felt only joy with her young son.

A Prayer at Valley Forge

This story about the Revolutionary War reminds us that in the worst of times, even great men need help. Often, they look to God to find it.

During the Revolutionary War, when Americans were fighting for their freedom, the British army captured Philadelphia. They marched into town with flags flying and bands playing, and made themselves at home for the winter. The fall of Philadelphia was a great blow to the Americans, for in those days it was the capital of the new nation.

But George Washington's army was not strong enough to stop the British forces. Once the king's men were inside the city, the only thing the American general could do was see that they did not get into the countryside to do any mischief. So Washington led his men to Valley Forge, a place just a few miles from Philadelphia. There the American army could spend the winter. It could defend itself if attacked, and it could keep close watch on the British.

It would have been easier to fight many battles than to spend that winter in Valley Forge. It was December, and there was no shelter of any kind. The soldiers bravely set to work building huts for themselves. They made them out of whatever they could find—logs, or fence rails, or just mud and straw. The snow drifted in at the windows, for they had no glass. The cold rain dripped through the roofs. The wind howled through every crack. There were few blankets, and many men slept shivering on the hard ground. Sometimes they sat up all night, crowding around the fires to keep from freezing.

Their clothing was worse than their shelter. The whole army was in rags. Many of the men had no shirts. Even more were without shoes. Wherever they walked, the snow was marked with their blood. Some cut strips from their precious blankets and wound them about their feet to protect them from the freezing ground.

Food was scanty. Sometimes for several days the soldiers went without meat. Sometimes they went even without bread. Around the camp, the groans of men who were sick and starving filled the air. Every evening, when the sun sank, the officers wondered if the army could hold together one more day.

One cold day a Quaker farmer was walking along a creek at Valley Forge when he heard the murmur of a solemn voice. Creeping in its direction, he discovered a horse tied to a tree, but no rider.

The farmer stole nearer, following the sound of the voice. Through a thicket, he saw a lone man, on his knees in the snow.

It was General Washington. His cheeks were wet with tears as he prayed to the Almighty for help and guidance.

The farmer quietly slipped away. When he reached home, he said to his wife, "Hannah, my dear! All is well! The Americans will win their independence! George Washington will succeed!"

"What makes thee think so, Isaac?" she asked.

"I have heard him pray, Hannah, out in the woods today," he said. "If there is anyone on this earth the Lord will listen to, it is this brave man. He will listen, Hannah. Rest assured, He will."

The farmer was right. When at last the harsh winter melted away, and a soft green crept over the hillsides, George Washington's army still lived. Against all odds, it had outlasted the cruel Valley Forge snows. With new hope the patriots marched away behind their brave commander, to fight the British and win their freedom.

Only a Dad

— EDGAR GUEST

It's not necessarily the big, famous deeds we admire the most. Sometimes, when we pause to appreciate a whole life—all the work, and love, and patient sacrifices for others—we suddenly discover a hero.

Only a dad with a tired face,
Coming home from the daily race,
Bringing little of gold or fame
To show how well he has played the game;
But glad in his heart that his own rejoice
To see him come and to hear his voice.

Only a dad with a brood of four,
One of ten million men or more
Plodding along in the daily strife,
Bearing the whips and the scorns of life,
With never a whimper of pain or hate,
For the sake of those who at home await.

Only a dad, neither rich nor proud,
Merely one of the surging crowd,
Toiling, striving from day to day,
Facing whatever may come his way,
Silent whenever the harsh condemn,
And bearing it all for the love of them.

Only a dad but he gives his all,
To smooth the way for his children small,
Doing with courage stern and grim
The deeds that his father did for him.
This is the line that for him I pen:
Only a dad, but the best of men.

The Fairy
Tale

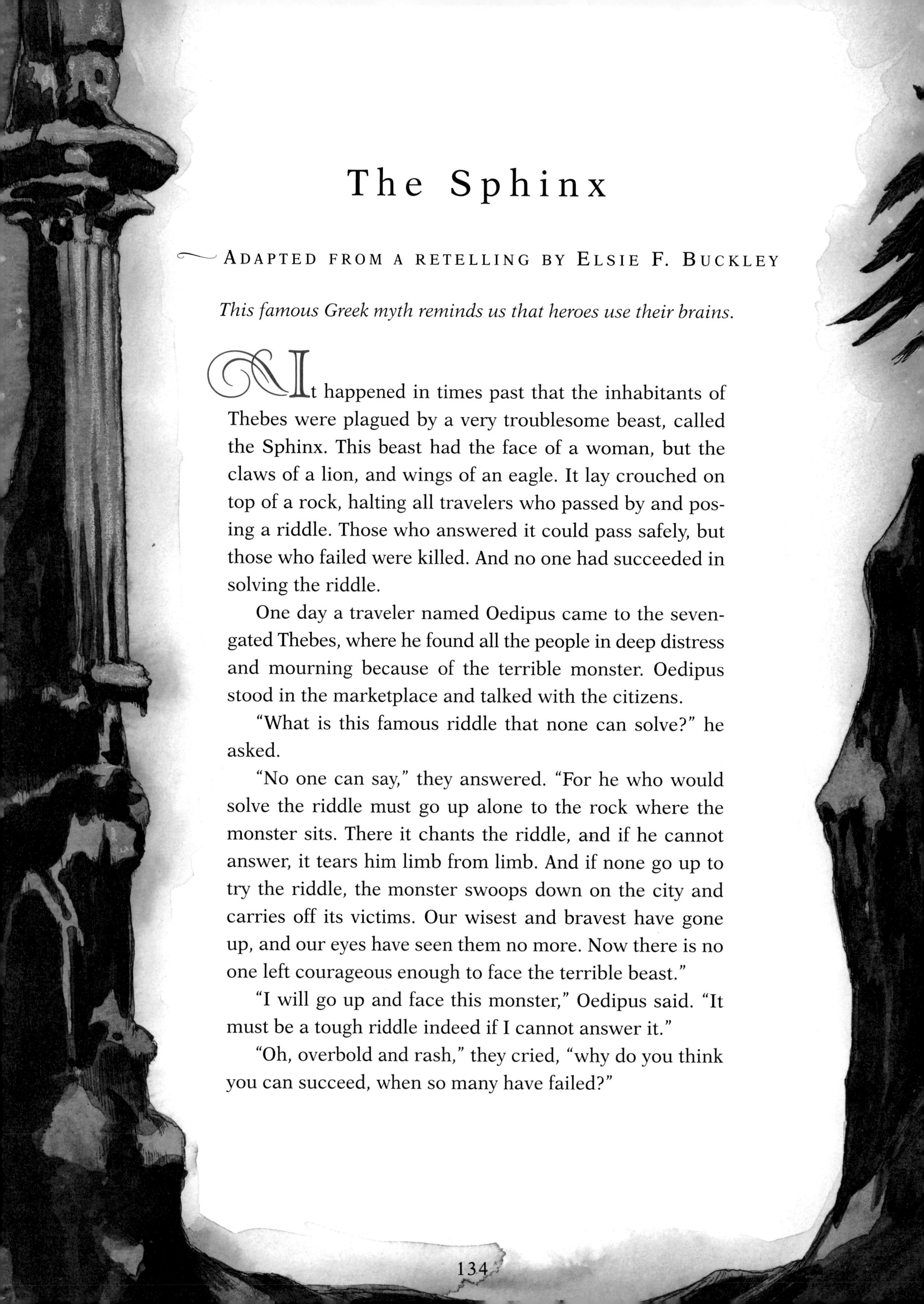

The Sphinx

ADAPTED FROM A RETELLING BY ELSIE F. BUCKLEY

This famous Greek myth reminds us that heroes use their brains.

It happened in times past that the inhabitants of Thebes were plagued by a very troublesome beast, called the Sphinx. This beast had the face of a woman, but the claws of a lion, and wings of an eagle. It lay crouched on top of a rock, halting all travelers who passed by and posing a riddle. Those who answered it could pass safely, but those who failed were killed. And no one had succeeded in solving the riddle.

One day a traveler named Oedipus came to the seven-gated Thebes, where he found all the people in deep distress and mourning because of the terrible monster. Oedipus stood in the marketplace and talked with the citizens.

"What is this famous riddle that none can solve?" he asked.

"No one can say," they answered. "For he who would solve the riddle must go up alone to the rock where the monster sits. There it chants the riddle, and if he cannot answer, it tears him limb from limb. And if none go up to try the riddle, the monster swoops down on the city and carries off its victims. Our wisest and bravest have gone up, and our eyes have seen them no more. Now there is no one left courageous enough to face the terrible beast."

"I will go up and face this monster," Oedipus said. "It must be a tough riddle indeed if I cannot answer it."

"Oh, overbold and rash," they cried, "why do you think you can succeed, when so many have failed?"

"Better to try and fail than never to try at all."

"Yet, where failure is death, surely a man should think twice?"

"A man can die but once, and how better than in trying to save his fellows?"

They marveled at his answer, and seeing that nothing would turn him from his purpose, they showed him the path to the Sphinx's rock. All the people went with him to the edge of the city with their prayers and blessings. At the gate they left him, for he who goes up to face the Sphinx must go alone, and none can stand by to help him.

He crossed first a river and then a wide plain, where the mountain of the Sphinx stood dark and clear on the other side. Then he prayed to Pallas Athena, the gray-eyed goddess of wisdom, and she took all fear from his heart.

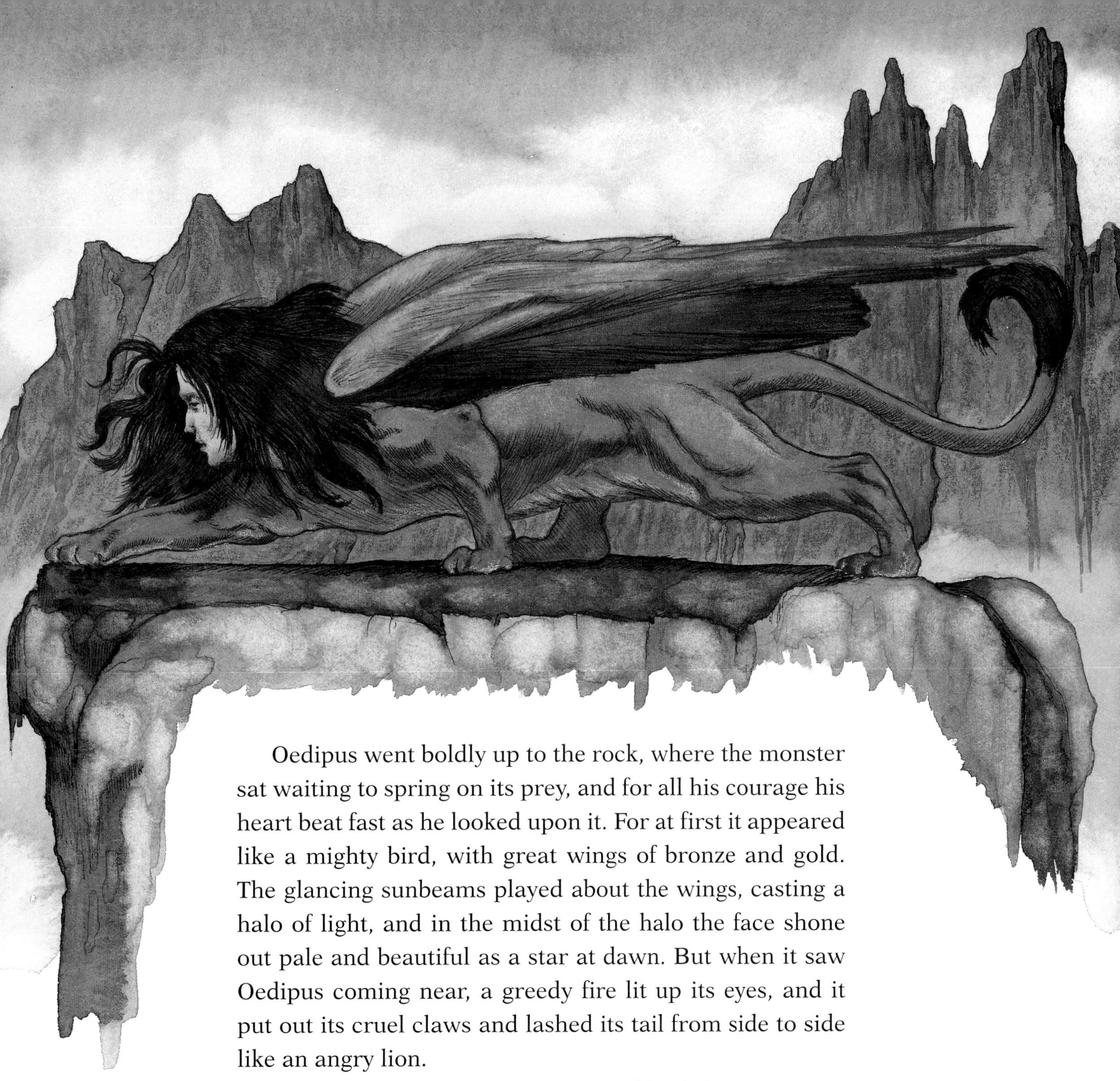

Oedipus went boldly up to the rock, where the monster sat waiting to spring on its prey, and for all his courage his heart beat fast as he looked upon it. For at first it appeared like a mighty bird, with great wings of bronze and gold. The glancing sunbeams played about the wings, casting a halo of light, and in the midst of the halo the face shone out pale and beautiful as a star at dawn. But when it saw Oedipus coming near, a greedy fire lit up its eyes, and it put out its cruel claws and lashed its tail from side to side like an angry lion.

Nevertheless, Oedipus spoke steadily. "I have come to hear your famous riddle and answer it or die."

"Foolhardy manling, a dainty morsel the gods have sent this day, with your fair young face and fresh young limbs."

And it licked its cruel lips.

Then Oedipus felt his blood boil within him, and he wished to slay it then and there.

"Come, tell me your famous riddle, foul Fury that thou art, that I may answer it and rid the land of this curse."

And this is what the monster asked: "At dawn it creeps on four legs. At noon it strides on two. At sunset and evening it totters on three. What is this thing, never the same, yet not many, but one?"

It chanted slowly, its eyes gleaming cruel and cold.

Oedipus thought to himself. "Now or never must my learning and wit stand me in good stead, or in vain have I talked with the wisest men and learned the old secrets of Phoenicia and Greece."

The gods who had given him understanding sent light into his heart, and he boldly answered: "What can this creature be but man, O Sphinx? For, a helpless babe at the dawn of life crawls on his hands and feet. At noontime he walks erect in the strength of his youth. And at evening he supports his tottering limbs with a staff, the prop and stay of old age. Have I not guessed the answer to your famous riddle?"

With a loud cry of despair, and answering him never a word, the great beast sprang up from its seat on the rock and hurled itself over the precipice into the yawning gulf below.

Far away across the plain the people heard its cry, and they saw the flash of the sun on its brazen wings like a gleam of lightning in the summer sky. They sent up a great shout of joy to heaven, and poured out from every gate onto the open plain. Some raised Oedipus on their shoulders and with shouts and songs bore him into the city. Then and there they made him their monarch, for who better to lead them than the slayer of the Sphinx and the savior of the city?

So Oedipus became king of Thebes, and wisely and well did he rule, and for many a long year the land prospered.

Jackie Robinson

Here is the story of an American hero who won his fight using self-control. Often, bravery means keeping your cool and doing the best you can in a bad situation.

More than anything else, Jackie Robinson loved to play baseball. And he was good at it. In fact, he was great. He could run like lightning, and he could hit the ball a mile. And like any other young player, he dreamed of playing baseball in the big leagues, in front of thousands of cheering fans.

But there was one big problem. The year was 1945, and Jackie Robinson was black. It was a time in America when black people were not allowed to do many things that white people could do. That was the rule in baseball too. Black people were not allowed to play on major league teams. They had their own baseball leagues, called the Negro leagues. Jackie played for a Negro league team called the Kansas City Monarchs.

But one day the man who ran a major league team called the Brooklyn Dodgers asked Jackie to come and see him. His name was Branch Rickey.

"I've heard what a good player you are," Mr. Rickey said. "I want you to play for our team."

Jackie could barely believe it. Would he really be the first black baseball player to make it to the big leagues?

"This will not be easy," Mr. Rickey went on. "There will be many, many people who will not want you to play for the Dodgers. Some of the players will call you dirty names. There will be fans in the stands who will yell awful things at you. Even some of the umpires will be against you, and will not give you fair calls."

"I can take it," Jackie said.

"You have to do more than that," Mr. Rickey told him. "You'll have to take it quietly. You cannot shout back. You cannot lose your temper and get into a fight. That's just what they want you to do. It will give them an excuse to throw you out of baseball. No, you must have the guts to fight back another way. The only way you can win this fight is by keeping your temper, and playing the best baseball you can.

You have to show them what a great player you are. That's how you will win this fight."

Jackie thought it over. It would not be an easy thing to do. At last he looked Mr. Rickey straight in the eye.

"I'll do it," he said. "I promise."

Mr. Rickey sent him to practice for a while with a Dodger farm team called the Montreal Royals. Every bad thing that Mr. Rickey had talked about came true—and more. Some of the other players said ugly things to him. Some refused to stand on the same field with him. Newspapers claimed he would not be able to play baseball well enough to stay on a white team. He was locked out of ballparks. In one town, a policeman even threatened to arrest him if he did not leave the field.

These things hurt Jackie's feelings deeply. Sometimes they made him so angry he wanted to raise his fists and strike back. But he remembered the promise he had made, and he kept his cool.

During Jackie Robinson's first game as a Montreal Royal, all eyes were on him. He knew how much was riding on that game, and it made him feel weak in the knees. But when his turn came, he stepped up to the plate and swung with all his might. The crowd heard the crack of the bat and watched the ball fly—and fly—and fly—right over the outfield wall. Jackie rounded the bases, and everyone knew then that he had come to play great baseball.

The next year, Jackie went to play with the Dodgers. He was in the big leagues at last! But his troubles did not end. In fact, they got only worse. Fans jeered him, and even threatened to harm him. Pitchers threw balls straight at him, trying to hit him. Players shoved him on the field or stepped on his feet at first base, where he played. But through it all, Jackie stayed calm and played great baseball.

One day, one of Jackie's teammates, a shortstop named Pee Wee Reese, trotted across the field to chat with Jackie. He put a friendly hand on Jackie's shoulder while he talked, and a photographer took a picture of the two men together. Newspapers all over the country carried the shot. The message was clear. There were white players who liked Jackie, and knew he was a great player, and were ready to have him on their team. They did not care about the color of his skin.

The more Jackie played, the more respect he won. There were still plenty of people who gave Jackie trouble simply because he was black. But as more and more people watched him play, they saw that he was good enough to be on any team. At the end of his first year with the Dodgers, Jackie was named Rookie of the Year—the best new player in the league.

He had shown the world that the color of his skin did not matter. What mattered was his skill with the bat and the ball, and his courage to lead the way.

B
Dodgers

Sail On! Sail On!

~ Joaquin Miller

Sometimes being a hero means having the courage and determination to say, "Forward!" while the crowd all around you cries, "Turn back!"

Behind him lay the gray Azores,
Behind the gates of Hercules;
Before him not the ghost of shores,
Before him only shoreless seas.
The good mate said: "Now must we pray,
For lo! the very stars are gone;
Speak, Admiral, what shall I say?"
"Why say, sail on! and on!"

"My men grow mut'nous day by day;
My men grow ghastly wan and weak."
The stout mate thought of home; a spray
Of salt wave wash'd his swarthy cheek.
"What shall I say, brave Admiral,
If we sight naught but seas at dawn?"
"Why, you shall say, at break of day:
'Sail on! sail on! and on!'"

They sailed and sailed, as winds might blow,
Until at last the blanch'd mate said:
"Why, now, not even God would know
Should I and all my men fall dead.
These very winds forget their way,
For God from these dread seas is gone.
Now speak, brave Admiral, and say—"
He said: "Sail on! and on!"

They sailed, they sailed, then spoke his mate:
"This mad sea shows his teeth tonight,
He curls his lip, he lies in wait,
With lifted teeth as if to bite!
Brave Admiral, say but one word;
What shall we do when hope is gone?"
The words leaped as a leaping sword:
"Sail on! sail on! and on!"

Then, pale and worn, he kept his deck,
And thro' the darkness peered that night.
Ah, darkest night! and then a speck—
A light! a light! a light! a light!
It grew—a star-lit flag unfurled!
It grew to be Time's burst of dawn;
He gained a world! he gave that world
Its watchword: "On! and on!"

David and Goliath

ADAPTED FROM A RETELLING BY
J. BERG ESENWEIN AND MARIETTA STOCKARD

Here is one of the world's most beloved heroes, a boy who found his courage in his faith.

Long ago, in the land of Bethlehem, there lived a shepherd boy named David. David was young, but he was also brave. His eye was keen and his hands were strong. Sometimes fierce, wild beasts would creep up the hillside where David watched his sheep, and try to seize a lamb. Then David would rush forward to defend his flock. Sometimes he took his sling and hurled a stone at the beast, and he never missed his mark.

There came a time when the army of the Philistines came marching across the hills to drive the people of Israel away from their homes. King Saul gathered his own army and went out to meet them. David's three oldest brothers went with the king, but David was left at home to tend the sheep. "You are too young," they told him. "Stay in the fields and keep the flocks safe."

Forty days went by, and no news of the battle came. Then David's father called him and said, "Take this food to your brothers in the camp, and see how they are doing."

David set out early in the morning and journeyed up to the hill where King Saul's army was camped. There was a great shouting between the army of the Israelites and army of the Philistines when David arrived. He made his way through the ranks and found his brothers.

As he stood talking with them, silence fell upon King Saul's army. For there on the opposite hillside, where the Philistine army lay, stood a great giant. He strode up and down, his armor glittering in the sun. His shield was as large as a great chariot wheel, and the sight of his mighty sword slashing the air struck terror in the hearts of King Saul's men.

"It is the great giant Goliath," David's brothers told him. "Each day he strides over the hill and calls out his challenge to the men of Israel, but no man among us dares to stand before him."

"What! Are the men of Israel afraid?" asked David. "Will no one go to meet him? Then I will go forth and meet this giant myself. I have no fear of him, for I know God will go with me."

King Saul heard about his words and called David. When he saw that David was only a boy, he tried to talk him out of facing the giant alone. But David had no fear.

"The Lord will keep me safe," he told Saul.

"Very well," said King Saul. "Go, and the Lord be with you!"

Then the king ordered his guards to bring his very own armor and sword for David. But David said, "I cannot fight with these. I am not skilled in their use." He put them down, for he knew that each man must win his battles with his own weapons.

Then he took his staff in his hand. With his shepherd's bag and sling hanging at his side, he set out from the camp of Israel. He ran down the hillside and came to a stream. There he stooped and chose five smooth stones from the stream, which he dropped into his bag.

The army of King Saul watched in silent wonder from one hill, while the host of the Philistines watched from the other. The great giant saw David and strode out to meet him. When Goliath saw that it was only a boy coming, he stopped.

"Do the men of Israel mock me by sending a child against me?" he shouted. "Turn back, or I will give your flesh to the birds of the air and the beasts of the field!"

But David had no fear in his heart, for he knew that God was with him. He put his hand into his bag and took one of the stones from it. He fitted it into his sling, and his keen eye found the place in the giant's forehead that the helmet did not cover.

As Goliath rushed forth to meet David, the shepherd drew his sling, and with all the force of his strong right arm, he hurled the stone.

It whizzed through the air and struck Goliath's forehead. His huge body tottered—then fell crashing to the ground. As he lay with his face upon the earth, David ran swiftly to his side, drew forth the giant's own sword, and severed his huge head from his body.

As soon as the army of Israel saw this, they rose with a great shout and rushed down the hillside. When the Philistines saw their greatest warrior slain by this lad, they fled toward their own land, leaving their tents and all their riches behind.

David the shepherd boy became known throughout the land for his bravery and his faith, and years later he became the king of Israel.

Our Heroes

~ PHOEBE CARY

Seeing what is right and doing it, even though the world tempts you to do something else, is the mark of moral courage.

Here's a hand to the boy who has courage
To do what he knows to be right;
When he falls in the way of temptation,
He has a hard battle to fight.
Who strives against self and his comrades
Will find a most powerful foe.
All honor to him if he conquers.
A cheer for the boy who says "NO!"

There's many a battle fought daily
The world knows nothing about;
There's many a brave little soldier
Whose strength puts a legion to rout.
And he who fights sin single-handed
Is more of a hero, I say,
Than he who leads soldiers to battle
And conquers by arms in the fray.

Be steadfast, my boy, when you're tempted,
To do what you know to be right.
Stand firm by the colors of manhood,
And you will o'ercome in the fight.
"The right" be your battle cry ever
In waging the warfare of life,
And God, who knows who are the heroes,
Will give you the strength for the strife.

Honest Abe

Some people grow to be great heroes by doing small, good deeds.

When Abraham Lincoln was a young man in the river town of New Salem, Illinois, he took a job as a clerk in a general store. There he sold the kinds of items frontier settlers needed—everything from buttons and cloth to ax handles and gunpowder.

One day a woman came into the store to buy a few things. Abe bundled her purchases and added up the bill. It came to two dollars and six cents. The woman laid the coins on the counter and, taking her package, wished Abe a good day.

But that evening, when the young clerk closed the store and sat down to count the day's earnings, he discovered he had six cents more than he should. He had taken too much from one of his customers. He realized at once who it was.

"I made a mistake," he said to himself. "I made her pay six cents too much."

Now even in those days, six cents was not much money. Many clerks would have shrugged and forgotten it. Abe was too honest for that.

"The money must be paid back," he decided.

That would have been easy enough if the woman had lived just around the corner. But as Abe knew, she lived three miles outside of town. That did not matter. He locked the store and set out.

It was getting dark outside. The moon climbed the sky and peered down from the clouds at a lone figure trudging through fields and woods.

At last Abe arrived at his customer's house. He knocked on the door, explained what had happened, paid back the six cents, and walked home satisfied.

That was the way the young clerk treated people—he always dealt fair and square with friends and strangers. Stories about his character spread among the folk of New Salem. They spoke of Abe Lincoln with warm, admiring smiles.

And years later, after he became President of the whole United States, they liked to remember him by the nickname he had earned in their town—"Honest Abe."

How the Animals Got Sunlight

This Native American tale is about trying against the odds, even when others have already tried and failed. Such perseverance sometimes makes heroes.

Once this part of the world was continually dark, and all the animals kept fumbling around and knocking into one another, and they never knew where they were in such blackness. Finally they called a great council to decide how to solve the problem.

"What we need is light," the Owl said. The Owl presided over the meeting because he could see better in the dark than the other animals.

"That's right! We need light," everyone cried. "But where do we get it?"

"It's not an easy thing," the Owl warned. "They say there is light on the other side of the world. But that's a long way away. The journey will be dangerous. Whoever goes may well never come back."

"Then who should go?" everyone cried at once. "Who will risk the journey?"

There was a long silence. All the birds and beasts shuddered in the blackness.

At last they heard a lowly voice.

"I'll try," the Possum offered. "I have a long, bushy tail. I can wrap some light inside its fur and carry it home behind me."

So the Possum set out alone, traveling to the east. He walked for days and days across the black earth, never knowing where he really was, until finally he began to see a little glow in the sky.

He hurried toward it, and it grew lighter and lighter. Soon it was so bright it hurt his eyes, and he had to squint to keep it from blinding him. And even today, possums often close their eyes in narrow slits, so that they look as though they are sleeping.

Finally, when he'd gone all the way to the other side of the world, the Possum found the sun. He grabbed a piece as fast as he could and wrapped it up in his long, bushy tail, and turned for home.

But the journey home was just as long, of course, and the piece of sun was too hot and bright for poor Possum. It burned all the fur off his tail, and fell onto the ground. That's why, today, Possum's tail is long and bare.

"Possum tried and failed," all the animals cried when he came home in darkness. "Now we'll never have any light."

"I'll try now," offered the Vulture. "Maybe this journey calls for someone with wings."

So the Vulture flew east, and finally he came to the sun. He dived and snatched a piece of it in his claws.

"Possum tried to carry the sun with his tail and dropped it," he told himself. "I'll try carrying it on my head."

Vulture set the piece of sun on his head and turned for home, but the sun was so hot that before long it had burned away all the feathers on his crown. He grew dizzy and lost his way, and began wandering around and around until the piece of sun tumbled to the ground. That is why today a vulture's head is bald, and you'll still see him drifting in circles high overhead.

"Now we're truly finished," the animals cried when Vulture returned in darkness. "Possum and Vulture tried as best they could, but it wasn't enough."

"Maybe we need to try one more time," a tiny voice rose from the weeds. "I'll go this time."

"Who is that?" the animals asked. "Who said that?"

“It’s me, Old Lady Spider. I know I’m small and slow, but perhaps I’m the one who can make it.”

Before she started, she gathered a bit of wet clay, and with her eight tiny hands she made a little pot.

“Possum and Vulture had nothing to carry the sun in,” she said. “I’ll put it in this pot.”

Then she spun a thread and fastened the end to a rock.

“The sun’s bright light hurt Possum’s eyes, and its heat made Vulture so dizzy he lost his way,” she said. “But I’ll follow this thread home.”

So she set out, traveling east, spinning her thread behind her as she walked. When she reached the sun, she pinched off a small piece and put it in her clay pot. It was still so bright she could hardly see, but she turned and followed her thread home.

She came walking out of the 'east all aglow, looking like the sun itself. And even today, when Old Lady Spider spins her web, it looks like the rays of the rising sun.

She reached home at last. All the animals could see for the first time. They saw how tiny and old Spider was, and they wondered that she could make the journey alone. Then they saw how she had carried the sun in the little pot, and that was when the world learned to make pots out of clay and set them in the sun to dry.

But Old Lady Spider had had enough of being so close to the sun. That is why, today, she spins her web in the early morning hours, before the sun is too high and hot.

The Star Jewels

ADAPTED FROM THE BROTHERS GRIMM

This beautiful little story echoes the words we find in the Gospel of Matthew: "I was hungry and you gave me food. . . . I was naked and you clothed me."

A little girl once lived all alone with her old grandmother on the borders of a forest. They were so poor that they were scarcely able to buy food to eat or clothes to cover them.

"Never mind, Granny," the little girl would say. "Someday I will be big enough to work, and then I will earn so much that I will be able to buy everything that we need, and to give something to other poor folk as well."

One day the child went off into the forest to gather sticks. These she hoped to sell for a few pennies in the town over beyond the hill. She was to be gone all day, so she took with her into the forest a bit of bread, which was all they had left to eat.

It was winter, and the air was bitterly cold. The child wrapped her little shawl about her and ran on as fast as she could. She was hungry, but she intended to save her crust until after the sticks were gathered.

Just as she reached the edge of the forest she met a boy even smaller than herself, and he was crying bitterly.

The little girl had a tender heart. She stopped and asked the child why he was weeping.

"I am weeping," he answered, "because I am hungry."

"Have you had nothing to eat today?" she asked.

"I have had nothing, and I am starving, for I do not know where to go for food."

The little girl sighed. "You are probably hungrier than I am," she said, and she took the crust from her pocket and gave it to the boy. Then she again hurried on.

A little farther on, she met another child, who was even more miserable looking than the first, for this child seemed almost frozen with cold. Her clothing hung about her in rags, and her skin looked blue through the holes.

"Ah," cried she, "if I had but a warm little dress like yours! Help me, I pray you, or I will certainly die of cold."

The good little girl was filled with pity. "I have both a dress and a shawl," she thought. "I will give one of them to this poor child."

She took off her dress and gave it to the child, and then wrapped the shawl closely about her shoulders. In spite of the shawl she felt very cold. Still, she was near the place where the sticks were to be found, and as soon as she had gathered them, she would run home again.

She hastened on, but when she reached the place where the sticks were, she saw an old woman already there, gathering up the fallen wood. The old woman was so bent and poor and miserable looking that the little girl's heart ached for her.

"Oh, oh!" groaned the old woman. "How my poor bones do ache. If I had but a shawl to wrap about my shoulders I would not suffer so."

The child thought of her own grandmother and of how she sometimes suffered, and she took pity on the old woman.

"Here," said she. "Take my shawl," and slipping it from her shoulders, she gave it to the old woman.

And now she stood there in the forest with her arms and shoulders bare, and with nothing on her but her little shift. The sharp wind blew about her, but she was not cold. She had eaten nothing, but she was not hungry. She was fed and warmed by her own kindness.

She gathered her sticks and started home again. It was growing dark and the stars shone through the bare branches of the trees. Suddenly an old man stood beside her. "Give me your sticks," said he, "for my hearth is cold, and I am too old to gather wood for myself."

The little girl sighed. If she gave him the sticks she would have to stop to gather more. Still, she would not refuse him. "Take them," she said, "in heaven's name."

No sooner had she said this than she saw it was not an old man who stood before her, but a shining angel.

"You have fed the hungry," said the angel. "You have clothed the naked, and you have given help to those who asked it. You shall not go unrewarded. See!"

At once a light shone around the child, and it seemed to her that all the stars of heaven were falling through the bare branches of the trees. But these stars were diamonds and rubies and other precious stones. They lay thick upon the ground. "Gather them together," said the angel, "for they are yours."

Wondering, the child gathered them together—all that she could carry in the skirt of her little shift.

When she looked about her again, the angel was gone, and the child hastened home with her treasure. It was enough to make her and her old grandmother rich. From then on they lacked for nothing. They were able not only to have all they wished for, but to give to many who were poor. So they were not only rich, but beloved by all who knew them.

Mother Teresa

Great heroes aren't only in stories of old and history books. They live and breathe and walk among us. Here is a modern-day heroine who has devoted her life to helping the needy all over the world.

In faraway India, in a city called Calcutta, there lives a woman named Mother Teresa. She is a small woman. Her back is bent with age. Her hands are rough from a lifetime of toil. Her face is wrinkled, but her eyes are steady and bright.

Mother Teresa is a nun, a woman of God. She lives in a large house with other women, who call one another "Sister," for they are like a family. They all have given their lives to God and try to do His work.

If you could go visit Mother Teresa and spend a day with her, what would you see?

She rises from bed very early in the morning, long before the sun rises. She says her prayers, eats her breakfast, and does her chores with the sisters. Then she leaves her house and goes into the streets.

Follow her, and you will see her walk into parts of the city where the buildings are dirty, the streets are full of trash, and the people wear sad, tired looks on their faces. She sees a child, perhaps no older than you, sitting against the wall. His clothes are ragged and his face is covered with dirt. He does not have a home. He does not know where his parents are.

Mother Teresa stops. She takes him by the hand. She wipes the dirt off his face and the tears from his eyes. She leads him to a place where the sisters will give him a bath and new clothes. Then they will try to find a family who will love him and take him into their home.

"A child is a gift of God," Mother Teresa says.
"Every child is here to love and be loved."

Follow Mother Teresa now as she walks more streets. She goes to the house of a woman who is sick. This woman has nobody to care for her. No one wants to come near her, for fear of catching her sickness. Mother Teresa bends over her bed. She gives her some medicine. She washes the places where her skin shows signs of disease. Then she cleans the poor woman's room and opens the windows to let in the fresh air.

"God has given us each a lighted lamp," Mother Teresa says. "It is our job to keep it burning. We can keep it burning only by pouring oil inside. That oil comes from our own acts of love."

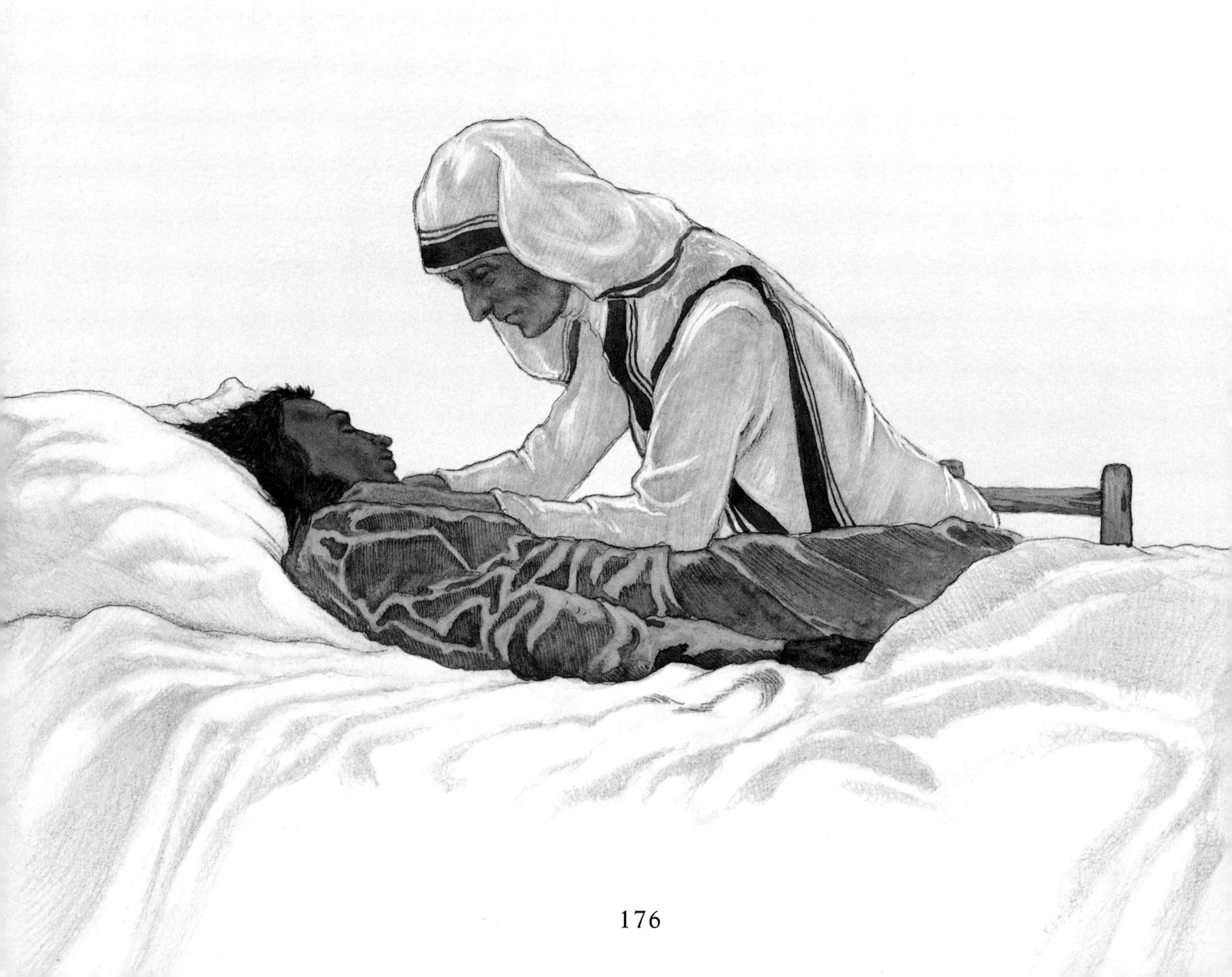

Follow Mother Teresa farther, and watch her go to the house of a family that has not eaten all day. The children's faces are thin from hunger. Mother Teresa gives this family some rice, and their eyes light up. Then the mother of the family does something wonderful. She takes the rice and divides it into two parts. She takes one half and carries it to the family next door.

"They are hungry, too," she tells Mother Teresa.

Mother Teresa smiles. "We call these people poor," she says, "but they are rich in love!"

Follow Mother Teresa just a little while longer, and you see her walk up to an old, old man in the street. He too looks sad and tired.

Mother Teresa lays a hand on his shoulder. "How are you doing?" she asks kindly.

The stranger is surprised, but his face lights up in a smile.

"It has been so long since I felt the warmth of another's hand!" he cries. "It has been so long since anyone cared to speak to me!"

Mother Teresa talks to him for a while, giving him comfort.

"The worst hunger of all is the hunger for love," she tells you as she walks on her way. "The worst sickness is the feeling that no one wants you."

If you came back another day and followed Mother Teresa again, you might see her get on a plane and fly far away, to other lands. You might see her visit the people of a country where there has been a terrible earthquake. You might see her travel to a place torn by war. Or you might find her visiting some of the sisters who do the same kind of work in their own countries as Mother Teresa does in India.

If you could travel with Mother Teresa, you would see that a wonderful thing has happened. You would meet many people who have seen what Mother Teresa is doing. They have seen her helping the poor and the sick, one person at a time. And they have decided to act like Mother Teresa. In their own countries, in their own cities, they take care of people who have no one else to help them. These are the Missionaries of Charity. You can find them all over the world.

And so this one little woman who walks the streets in India, trying to help one person at a time, has really helped thousands and thousands of people all over the world. It is a kind of miracle.

If you ask Mother Teresa, she will tell you that it is not her doing. "It is God's work that has been done, not my work," she says. "I am just God's pencil. That is all I am. I am His tiny pencil, and He writes through me. He uses me to write what He likes."

She smiles as she tells you good-bye. But she stops to say one more thing. What is it she wants to tell you? It is this.

"Let everything you do be something beautiful for God," she says.

The Knights of the Silver Shield

— Raymond M. Alden

Sometimes being a hero means resisting the call to glory elsewhere and standing fast at your post.

Once in a land far away there was a dark and dangerous forest, where many cruel giants lived. But in the middle of this forest stood a splendid castle. And inside the castle lived a company of knights, who fought the cruel giants whenever they could.

Each of these knights had a silver shield that did something quite wonderful. When a new knight first received his shield, its surface looked cloudy and dull. As the knight began to do service against the giants, his shield grew brighter and brighter, until he could see his face reflected on its surface. But if the knight proved to be lazy or cowardly, his shield grew more and more cloudy, until he became ashamed to carry it.

But this was not all. When any one of the knights won a very great victory, not only did his silver shield grow brighter, but anyone looking into its center could see something like a golden star shining in its very heart. Winning his star was the greatest honor a knight could achieve.

There came a time when the giants in the forest gathered themselves together to battle the knights. All the knights in the castle made ready to go out and fight them.

Now, there was one young knight named Sir Roland. Though he was still quite young, his shield had already begun to shine enough to show that he was brave. He could not wait to ride forth and battle the giants, to prove what knightly stuff he was made of.

But the lord of the castle came to him and said: "One brave knight must stay behind and guard the castle gate. Since you are the youngest, I have chosen you, Sir Roland."

Sir Roland was so disappointed that he bit his lip and closed his helmet over his face so the other knights would not see it. For a moment he felt as if he must reply angrily to the commander and tell him it was not right to leave so sturdy a knight behind. But he struggled against this feeling and went quietly to look after his duties at the gate.

Soon all the other knights marched out in their flashing armor. The lord of the castle stopped only to give Sir Roland the key to the gate. He told him to keep guard until they all returned, and to let no one enter. Then the knights rode into the shadows of the forest and were lost to sight. Sir Roland stood looking after them unhappily.

A long time passed. At last Sir Roland saw one of the knights come riding along the path to the castle, and he walked out on the drawbridge to meet him.

"I have been hurt and cannot fight anymore," said the knight. "I can watch the gate for you, if you would like to go back in my place."

At first Sir Roland's heart leaped with joy. But then he thought better, and he said:

"I would like to go, but a knight belongs where his commander has put him."

The knight was ashamed when he heard this, and he turned around and went back into the forest.

Sir Roland kept guard silently for another hour, worrying about his friends. Then an old woman came down the path to the castle, and stopped to rest on the other side of the moat.

"I have been past the hollow in the forest where the battle is going on," she called. "The knights are faring badly. I think you had better go help your friends."

"I would like to go," Sir Roland answered, "but I am set to guard the castle gate, and I cannot leave."

"Oh, I see." The old woman laughed. "You are one of the kind of knights who like to keep out of the fighting. You are lucky to have so good an excuse for staying home."

Sir Roland was angry then and wanted to go help his friends more than ever. But instead he shut the gate so he would not have to hear the old woman's laughs.

It was not long before he heard someone else calling outside. He opened the gate and saw standing at the other end of the drawbridge a little old man in a long black cloak.

"Sir Roland!" he called. "You should not be wasting time here when the knights are having such a hard struggle against the giants. Listen to me! I have brought you a magic sword."

And he drew from under his cloak a wonderful sword that flashed as if it were covered with diamonds. "Nothing can stand before this sword!" he called. "Take it into battle, and when you lift it the giants will fall back, and your friends will be saved!"

Sir Roland believed this man must be a friendly magician. He reached out his hand toward the sword, and the little old man started onto the drawbridge. But just then Sir Roland remembered his orders and cried out, "No!"

The little old man waved the sword in the air and cried, "But it is for you! Take it, and win the victory!"

Sir Roland was afraid that if he looked any longer, he would not be able to stay inside the castle. So at once he drew up the drawbridge.

Then, as he looked across the moat, he saw a wonderful thing. The little old man threw off his black cloak, and suddenly he began to grow bigger and bigger, until he was a giant as tall as any tree in the forest!

Sir Roland knew at once that this must be one of their giant enemies, who had changed himself into a little old man through some magic power, so that he might trick his way into the castle while the other knights were away. The giant shook his fist across the moat and went angrily back into the forest.

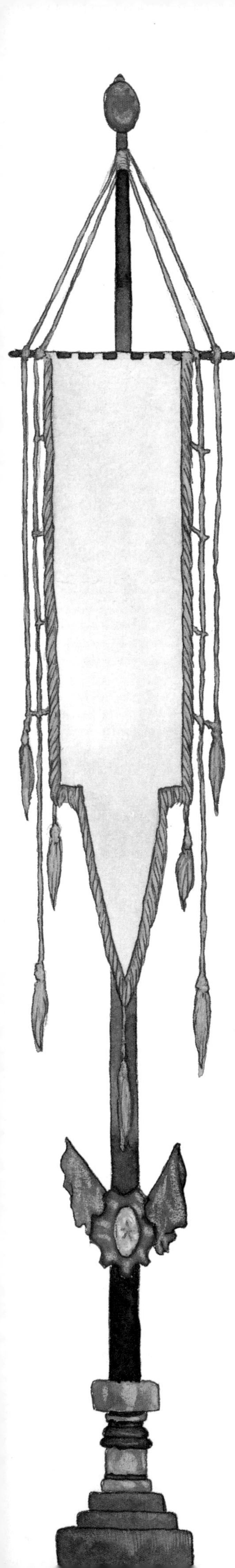

A moment later, Sir Roland heard his master's bugle and shouts of victory. The knights came riding back. They were dusty and bloodstained and weary, but they had won the battle.

Sir Roland greeted them all as they passed over the drawbridge, and then followed them into the great hall of the castle. The lord of the castle took his place on the highest seat, and Sir Roland came forward to return the key to the gate. As he approached, one of the knights cried out:

"The shield! Sir Roland's shield!"

For there, in the very center of Sir Roland's shield, shined the golden star!

"Speak, Sir Knight," said the commander, "and tell us all that has happened today at the castle. Have you been attacked? Did you fight the giants alone?"

"No, my lord," said Sir Roland. "Only one giant has been here, and he went away silently when he found he could not enter." Then he told them everything that had happened that day.

When he had finished, the knights all looked at one another, but no one spoke a word. At last the lord of the castle spoke.

"Men make mistakes," he said, "but our silver shields are never mistaken. Sir Roland has fought and won the hardest battle of all today."

The others rose and gladly saluted Sir Roland, who was the youngest knight who ever carried the golden star.

The Minotaur

These two brave heroes were afraid of the danger they faced—one can almost hear their hearts beating. They chose to do the right thing anyway.

Long ago, in ancient Greece, the city of Athens lived under a sad, cruel curse. Once every seven years, a ship with black sails entered its port. The ship came from the island of Crete, which was ruled by the great King Minos, the Athenians' dreaded enemy. Each time it came, the vessel took seven young men and seven young women from Athens, and then sailed away again.

A terrible fate awaited these poor captives when the black-sailed ship reached Crete. There King Minos kept a strange prison, a kind of maze, called the Labyrinth. It was full of dark winding ways, cut in the solid rock, and inside lived a horrible monster called the Minotaur. This monster had the body of a man, but his head was the head of a bull, his teeth the teeth of a lion, and he devoured everyone he met. It was the fate of the Athenian youth to be thrown into the Labyrinth, to meet the awful Minotaur.

Every seven years the black-sailed ship came and took its hostages. The Athenians did not dare resist, for King Minos had declared that if they tried, he would send his great army to destroy all of Athens.

But one year, when the awful time came again, a great hero joined the band of captives who boarded the sad ship. It was Theseus, the prince of Athens. He stood on the deck beneath the black sails, and he set his eyes straight ahead as the ship plowed across the water toward Crete. For he had sworn to free his countrymen from this awful curse, or die trying.

When the ship reached Crete at last, Theseus stood with the others before King Minos.

"Who are you?" Minos demanded.

"My name is Theseus," the hero replied. "I am the son of the king of Athens. I have come to ask you to let me face the Minotaur alone. If I slay him, you must trouble the people of Athens no longer. If I fail, my companions will follow me into the Labyrinth."

"The king's son wishes to die." Minos laughed. "Very well. You will face the Minotaur tomorrow."

Now, it happened that Minos's own daughter, a wise and tenderhearted girl named Ariadne, saw the look of courage in the eyes of Theseus. That night, she crept past her father's guards and gave the prince a dagger.

"This will help you face the Minotaur," she whispered. "But even if you are strong enough to kill the monster, you will need to find your way out of the Labyrinth. It is made of so many dark twists and turns that not even my father knows the secrets of its windings. So you must also take this with you."

She placed in his hand a spool of gold thread, and told him to tie one end to a stone as soon as he entered the Labyrinth." Hold tight to the spool as you wander through the maze," she said. "When you are ready to come back, the thread will be your guide."

"Why are you doing this?" Theseus asked. "If your father finds out, you will be in great danger."

"Yes," Ariadne answered slowly, "but if I do not help, you and your friends will be in far greater danger."

And Theseus knew then that he loved her.

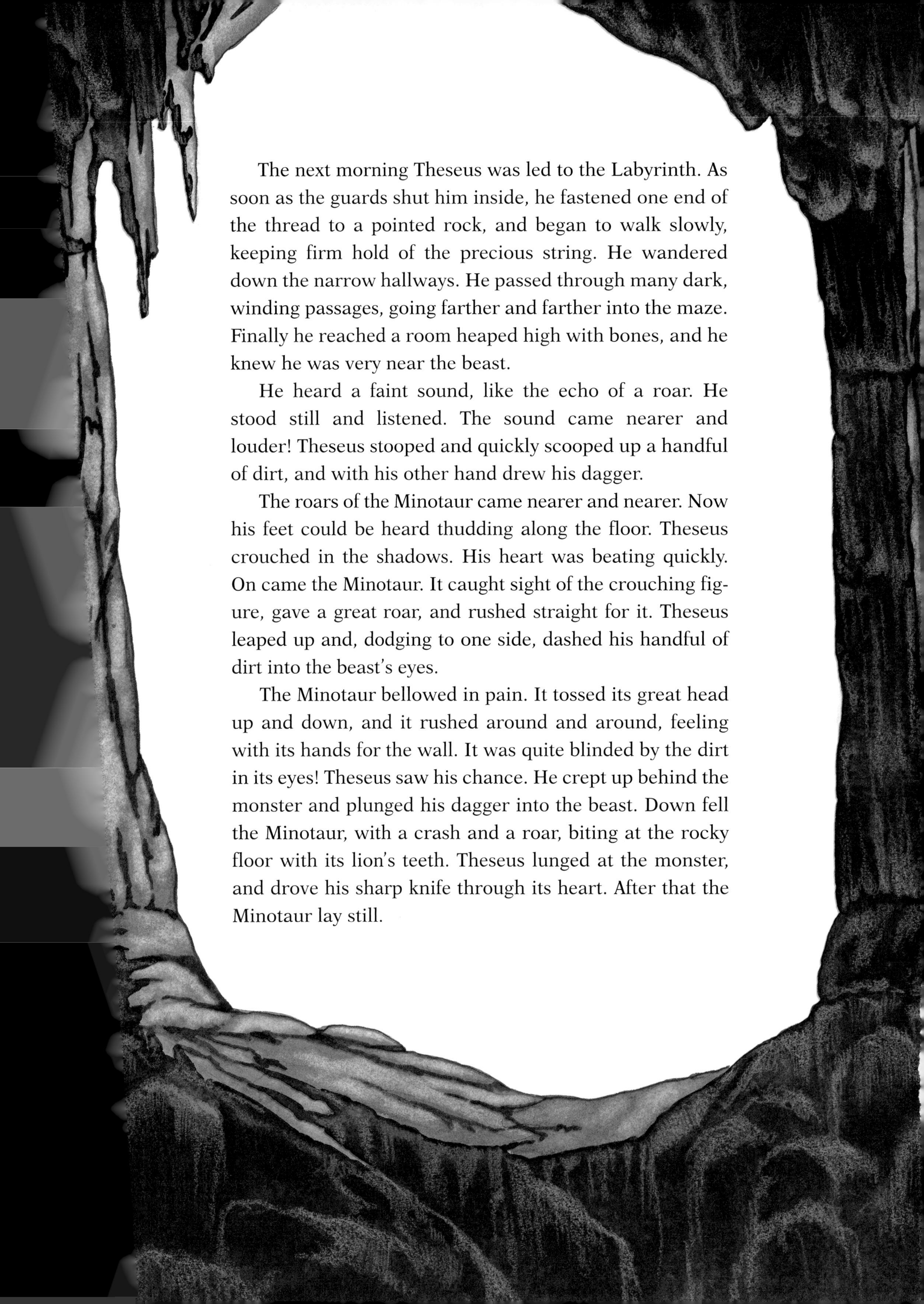

The next morning Theseus was led to the Labyrinth. As soon as the guards shut him inside, he fastened one end of the thread to a pointed rock, and began to walk slowly, keeping firm hold of the precious string. He wandered down the narrow hallways. He passed through many dark, winding passages, going farther and farther into the maze. Finally he reached a room heaped high with bones, and he knew he was very near the beast.

He heard a faint sound, like the echo of a roar. He stood still and listened. The sound came nearer and louder! Theseus stooped and quickly scooped up a handful of dirt, and with his other hand drew his dagger.

The roars of the Minotaur came nearer and nearer. Now his feet could be heard thudding along the floor. Theseus crouched in the shadows. His heart was beating quickly. On came the Minotaur. It caught sight of the crouching figure, gave a great roar, and rushed straight for it. Theseus leaped up and, dodging to one side, dashed his handful of dirt into the beast's eyes.

The Minotaur bellowed in pain. It tossed its great head up and down, and it rushed around and around, feeling with its hands for the wall. It was quite blinded by the dirt in its eyes! Theseus saw his chance. He crept up behind the monster and plunged his dagger into the beast. Down fell the Minotaur, with a crash and a roar, biting at the rocky floor with its lion's teeth. Theseus lunged at the monster, and drove his sharp knife through its heart. After that the Minotaur lay still.

Theseus breathed a sigh of relief, then took his dagger and cut off the monster's head. With this proof of victory, he followed the string through the winding, gloomy passages, until at last he came back to the beginning of the Labyrinth.

"I do not know what miracle caused you to come out of the Labyrinth alive," Minos said when he saw the monster's head, "but I will keep my word. I promised you freedom if you slew the Minotaur. You and your comrades may go."

Theseus knew he owed his life and his country's freedom to Ariadne's courage, and he knew he could not leave without her. Some say that he asked Minos for her hand in marriage, and the king gladly consented. Others say Ariadne stole onto the departing ship at the last minute without her father's knowledge. Either way, the two lovers were together when the anchor lifted and the dark ship sailed away from Crete.

Helen Keller's Teacher

Some of the luckiest boys and girls are the ones who have teachers as heroes.

Helen Keller was not like most little girls. She could not see the flowers blooming in her yard, or the butterflies floating from blossom to blossom, or the white clouds drifting in the high, blue sky. She could not hear the birds singing in the treetops outside her window, or the laughing and singing of other children at play. Little Helen was blind and deaf.

And because she could not hear people talking, Helen had never learned to speak. She could clutch her mother's dress and follow her around the house, but she did not know how to say to her, "I love you." She could climb into her father's lap, but she could not ask him, "Will you read me a story?" She lived in a dark, quiet world, where she felt all alone.

One afternoon when she was almost seven years old, Helen stood on her porch. She could feel a warm glow on her face, but she did not know it came from the sun. She smelled the sweetness of the honeysuckle vine growing beside her house, but she did not know what it was.

Suddenly Helen felt two arms wrap around her and hold her close. She knew at once it was not her mother or her father. At first she kicked and scratched and hit, trying to drive this stranger away. But then she began to wonder who it might be. She reached out and felt the stranger's face, then her dress, and then the big suitcase she carried with her.

How was Helen to understand that this young woman was Annie Sullivan, who had come to live with Helen and be her teacher?

Annie had brought a present. She gave Helen a doll. Then she put her fingers against Helen's hand, and made signs that Helen could feel. Annie slowly spelled D-O-L-L with her fingers. Helen felt Annie's fingers moving, but she did not know what this woman was trying to tell her. She did not understand that each of these finger signs was a letter, and that the letters spelled the word *doll*. She pushed Annie away.

The new teacher did not give up. She gave Helen a piece of cake, and spelled the word C-A-K-E against her hand. Helen made the signs with her own fingers, but still she did not understand what they meant.

Over the next days and weeks, Annie put many different things into Helen's hands, and spelled out the words. She tried to teach her words like *pin,* and *hat,* and *cup.* To Helen it all seemed very odd. She grew tired of this strange woman always taking her hand. Sometimes she grew angry with Annie, and began striking out at the darkness around her. She kicked and scratched. She screamed and growled. She broke plates and lamps.

Sometimes Annie wondered if she would ever be able to help little Helen break out of her lonely world of darkness and silence. But she promised herself she would not give up.

Then one morning Helen and Annie were walking outside when they passed an old well. Annie took Helen's hand and held it under the spout while she pumped. As the cold water rushed forth, Annie spelled W-A-T-E-R.

Helen stood still. In one hand she felt the cool, gushing water. In the other hand she felt Annie's fingers, making the signs over and over again. Suddenly a thrill of hope and joy filled her little heart. She understood that W-A-T-E-R meant the wonderful, cool something that was flowing over her hand. She understood at last what Annie had been trying to show her for days and weeks. She saw now that everything had a name, and that she could use her fingers to spell out each name!

Helen ran laughing and crying back to the house, pulling Annie along with her. She touched everything she could lay her hands on, asking for their names—*chair, table, door, mother, father, baby,* and many more. There were so many wonderful words to learn! But none was more wonderful than the word Helen learned when she touched Annie to ask her name, and Annie spelled T-E-A-C-H-E-R.

Helen Keller never stopped learning. She learned to read with her fingers, and how to write, and even how to speak. She went to school and to college, and Annie went with her to help her learn. Helen and Annie became friends for life.

Helen Keller grew up to be a great woman. She devoted her life to helping people who could not see or hear. She worked hard, and wrote books, and traveled across the seas. Everywhere she went, she brought people courage and hope. Presidents and kings greeted her, and the whole world grew to love her. A childhood that had begun in darkness and loneliness turned into a life full of much light and joy.

"And the most important day in my life," Helen said, "was the day my teacher came to me."

Father Flanagan

Here is the real-life story of a man who believed every boy needs a hero called father.

If you ever go to the state of Nebraska, you will find a very special town of children. The young citizens of this wonderful little village vote to elect their own mayor and council members, who might be boys or girls just a few years older than you. They hold their own court whenever someone breaks the rules. Like any city, their town has its own post office and fire station. It has schools, ball fields, movie theaters, and even its own town band.

This is the story of Father Flanagan, the man who founded such a marvelous place. He was born in Ireland, but when he was a young man he came to the United States to be a priest. His church was in Omaha, Nebraska, where our story begins.

Omaha had a problem—boys! Unlike most children, these boys had no mothers and fathers to look after them. Many of them had no homes, and no one to love them and show them right from wrong. And so, some of them got into trouble. They broke store windows, stole fruit from the grocer, and fought in the street.

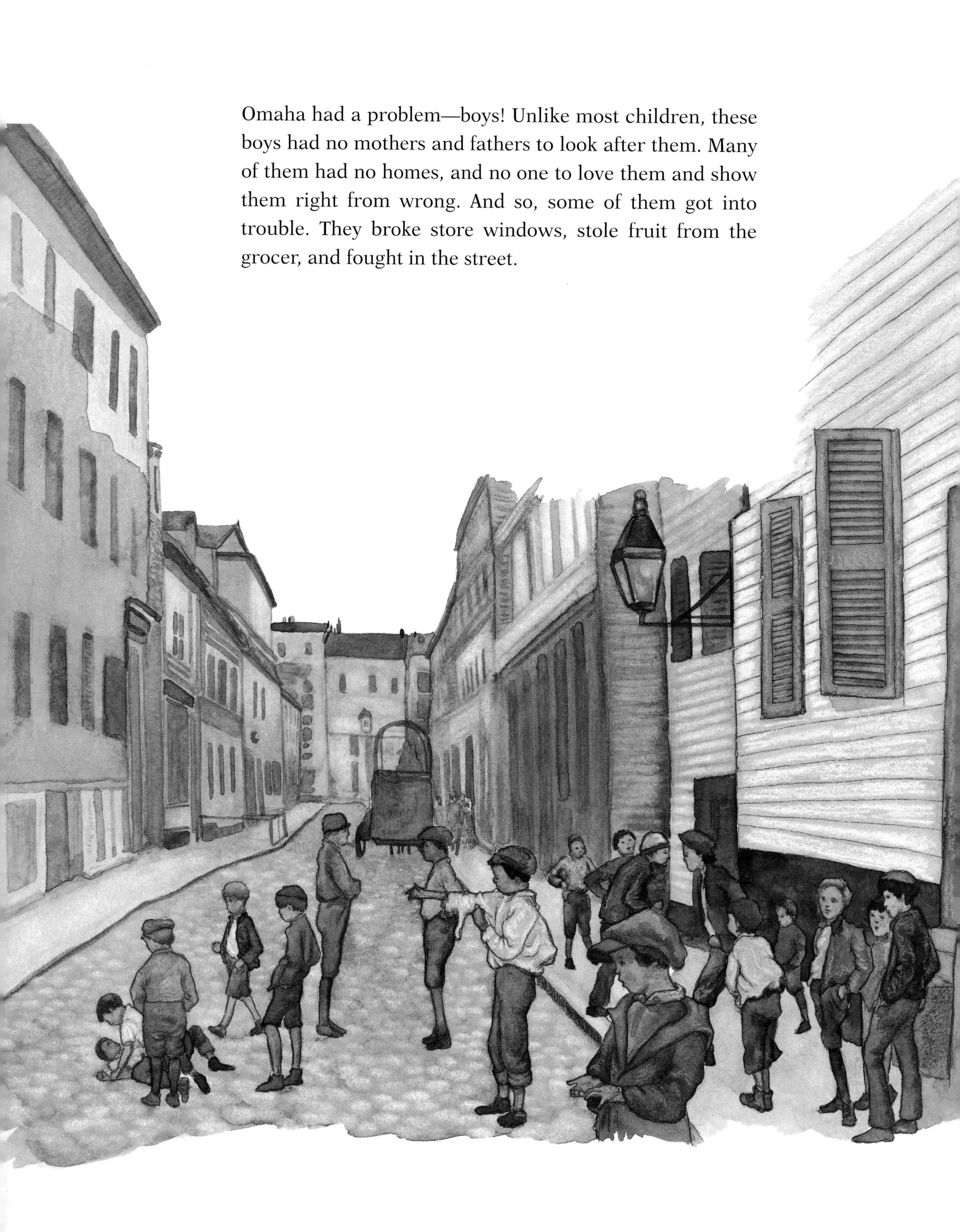

When Father Flanagan saw their hungry faces and ragged clothes, it broke his heart.

"Those boys should be arrested," said the grocer. "They need to be taken away."

Father Flanagan shook his head. "What they need is a home," he said. "They need someone to love them."

"But who would take them in?" asked the grocer.

"Maybe I will," said Father Flanagan.

And he did. He borrowed a few dollars to rent an old house, and trudged from door to door, asking for used furniture, plates, cups, spoons, blankets, rugs, and anything else his neighbors would give away. When he told people what he was doing, they thought he was crazy. But they also saw a kind, good man and gave him what they could.

He started with just five boys and gave them a place to eat, sleep, play, and pray. He gave them a home where they could feel safe and warm.

This was just what they needed. Before long they were laughing, learning, and growing up strong. When people saw what Father Flanagan was doing, they brought him more homeless and orphan boys. Before long he had outgrown his house and had to find a bigger one. But more and more boys came, and soon they had outgrown the new house too.

"These boys need a place all to themselves," thought Father Flanagan, "where they can run and play in fresh air, go to school and church, and grow up to be fine young men. They need a town of their own."

And that is just what Father Flanagan gave them. Outside of Omaha he found a farm for sale. He had no money to buy the land, but that did not stop him. Once again he went to friends and neighbors for help. When they heard what he had in mind, they were puzzled. A town for boys nobody wanted? Whoever heard of such a thing? But they knew that when Father Flanagan got an idea, he would never give up. So they pitched in to help him buy the farm and build his town.

Before too long, the streets and sidewalks of Boys Town covered the fields. Father Flanagan and his friends built houses and shops. They built a church and a post office. They built a big dining room where all the boys could eat and a pool where they could swim. And from all over the country, boys without mothers or fathers to take care of them came to Boys Town, where Father Flanagan gave them a home.

One day a boy who could not walk came to Boys Town. He was a tiny fellow, so Father Flanagan asked one of the bigger boys to carry him to his room. The big boy hoisted the newcomer onto his back.

"He's not too heavy, is he?" Father Flanagan asked.

"He ain't heavy, Father. He's my brother!" The older boy smiled.

And that was the best thing of all about Father Flanagan's Boys Town. The boys who came there found a family of hundreds of brothers who took care of each other, and a father who loved them all.

Boys Town is still there today, and if you ever go to Nebraska, you can visit it and see it for yourself. The wonderful town is still full of boys—and girls now, too—who have no parents to take care of them. You can see them laughing, playing, and studying their books, and growing up to be strong, good people. And when you see the smiles on their faces, you can remember the story of the father who built the town so many children have called home.

The Hero of Indian Cliff

—Adapted from C. H. Claudy

This is a story about true brotherhood, about putting yourself on the line for someone you love.

High above a valley floor, in the giant Rocky Mountains of Colorado, two brothers climbed a steep mountainside. Higher and higher they hiked, until it seemed they would reach the sky itself.

The older brother went first. He carried a knapsack of food, a canteen full of cold water, and a long coil of rope. Sometimes, when the trail grew very steep, he would tie the rope around a tree and throw the other end to his brother, to make it easier for him to follow.

"Get a good grip on the rope, Nando," he would call. "And watch where you plant your feet."

For a whole year, Nando had been waiting for this hike. Today he was nine years old. For a birthday present, his brother, Manuel, was finally showing him the way to a secret lookout—Indian Cliff!

Manuel was almost twelve, and he had been coming to Indian Cliff for two years now. He was sure of the path and could climb as quickly as a mountain goat. But today he went slowly, to help Nando along.

Sometimes Nando would try to climb too fast, and then he would lose his breath.

"Take your time, Nando," Manuel would say. "We'll get there soon enough."

Sometimes their feet knocked loose small stones, which went rolling down the mountain behind them. Nando could hear the echoes of the stones tumbling farther and farther away, crashing against trees or bouncing off boulders.

"Don't look down," Manuel would remind him. "Just keep your eyes on the trail."

Up and up they climbed. They passed behind a thundering waterfall. They hiked through woods where the trees clung to the rocks. They scrambled over ridges and inched their way through openings between huge boulders.

"I call this place Fat Man Squeeze." Manuel laughed, and Nando laughed too.

Finally they reached a place where the path grew level. They walked a short way through a forest. Then at once they left the trees and stepped into a small green meadow, perched on top of a towering cliff. It seemed as though the whole world lay at their feet.

Far, far below, Nando could see the valley where he lived. The highway running up the valley, the one his school bus followed every day, looked like nothing more than a thin black ribbon. His school seemed no bigger than a matchbox. Across the tiny woods and fields he could see his town, with its little streets and stores and steeples. And beyond the town lay more mountains, peak after peak capped with snow.

"This is it—my secret lookout," Manuel said. "I'll show you why I call it Indian Cliff." He reached into the hollow of a tree. When he pulled his hand out, it held three small sharp stones.

"Arrowheads!" Nando cried.

"Yeah. I found them lying on the trail," Manuel said proudly. "I think the Indians used to camp here."

The boys walked close to the edge of the cliff—but not too close—and found two rocks for seats. Manuel took sandwiches and apples from his knapsack, and they had lunch while they shared the view.

They ate without saying much. They did not want to spoil the wonderful silence that comes from being so far above the rest of the world. Together they watched the shadows of the clouds drifting across the valley floor, and followed the hawks and eagles floating far below them. They sat gazing for half an hour. At last Manuel stood up to stretch his legs.

Then it happened, without warning! The rock Manuel was using for a seat suddenly shifted. It slid down the slope toward the brink of the cliff, carrying Manuel with it!

Manuel gave a yell and spread out his arms, trying to catch hold of something. He felt himself sliding over the edge, and then falling. His feet struck a ledge, and he stopped—but at once the ledge crumbled away, and he felt himself sliding down again. His fingers grabbed on to a jagged bit of rock, and with a jerk he came to a halt.

He looked straight down and saw his legs dangling over empty space.

He was hanging from the side of Indian Cliff.

He did not try to move. In a flash he knew where his only hope lay.

"Nando!" he screamed. "The rope! Tie it around the arrowhead tree, and lower it down to me!"

Somewhere above he could hear Nando scrambling along the top of the cliff and calling down to him. A little bit of earth, loosened from above in some way, struck him gently on the shoulders and neck. What if a large amount should come down before Nando could get the rope to him?

"But it won't—I'm sure it won't. Nando will send the rope down in a minute—and then I'll get out of this mess," Manuel told himself. But then he had a horrible thought: *"What if the rope is not long enough to reach me?"*

Manuel's fingers ached. With each passing second, it grew harder and harder to hold on. He knew that any movement might cause him to lose his grip. But slowly, slowly he turned his head, and strained his eyes to look up. And far above, he caught sight of the end of the rope. Nando was lowering it down the cliff!

Manuel watched it come slowly down the rock face, twisting and turning like a long, thin snake. Moving slowly, sliding, catching on bits of rock and then dropping again, the end came gradually nearer. And then it stopped—just a few inches above Manuel's hands!

"It's no good!" Manuel yelled. "I can't reach it!"

A second later the rope rose a short way back up the cliff. It hung there for a moment, its end waving and shaking in the air. Then it started down again—and this time it reached Manuel with two feet to spare.

Manuel held his breath, got a firm grip, and slowly began to pull himself up. He pulled with his arms, and pushed with his legs by sticking his feet into cracks in the cliff. Halfway up he had a terrible scare—the rope seemed to give a little, and at the same time he heard a cry from Nando somewhere above.

Now Manuel was only five feet from the top—now three feet—only one foot to go—now safety! With a shout of joy he pulled himself onto the top of the cliff.

At once he saw what Nando had done. His little brother lay on his stomach, his arms locked tight around the arrowhead tree. The rope was knotted around one of his ankles. There had not been enough rope to reach Manuel, so Nando had made it longer with his own body!

Manuel fell on the ground beside Nando, put one arm around his neck, and burst into sobs of relief. In a moment Nando sat up, and his face was shining with joy.

Nando's ankle was bruised and raw from the rope. Manuel helped him stand up and told him to lean on his arm. Together they started back down the trail toward home.

"I was scared, Manuel, real scared," Nando said.

"I know," Manuel answered. "I was scared too."

They walked slowly, helping each other along.

"And I know one more thing," Manuel said. "I'll never come back to Indian Cliff without my little brother to look after me."

Tashira's Turn

The small, daily examples of others can turn any one of us into a hero.

One day Tashira ran outside for recess and found her mother on the edge of the school yard with a bucket of soap and water. She was scrubbing a wall where someone had painted some ugly words and pictures. She scrubbed as hard as she could.

"Mama!" Tashira called. "What are you doing here?"

"Oh, I'm just helping your teachers keep the school clean," her mother said.

"It looks like hard work," said Tashira.

"It's nothing at all." Her mother smiled. "It's just my turn to help, you see."

The school bell rang. Tashira's teacher looked out the door and waved. Tashira's mom waved back, and went back to scrubbing the wall. All the ugly words and pictures ran to the ground, where they turned into puddles of silver and gold.

The next morning Tashira was walking past her church, when she heard voices singing in the sky. She looked straight up, and saw her teacher on the roof!

"Hello, Mrs. Jenkins," Tashira called. "What are you doing way up there?"

"We're helping our friend Reverend Wilburn," her teacher called down. "The steeple needs a fresh coat of paint."

"That's very brave of you to climb so high," Tashira shouted.

"It's not so very high," her teacher sang out. "Besides, it's our turn to help today."

Reverend Wilburn stepped out the church door and waved to his friends on the roof. Tashira's teacher waved her paintbrush back, and it looked as if she were painting the clouds in the sky.

The next morning, Tashira was skipping rope when she saw Reverend Wilburn with a basket under his arm.

"Hello, Reverend Wilburn," she called. "Where are you going with that great big basket?"

"I'm taking dinner to Officer Hamlette and his family." Reverend Wilburn smiled. "Mrs. Hamlette just had a new baby. Everyone in the church is taking turns sending a meal. Doesn't that smell good?" He lifted the basket's cover so Tashira could peek inside.

"It's very kind of you to cook such a nice, juicy turkey," she said.

"Oh, it's just my turn to help, that's all," said Reverend Wilburn.

He carried his basket up some steps and knocked four times. Officer Hamlette opened the door and smiled. Everyone on the street knew Officer Hamlette because he wore such a big, shiny badge. Inside the house, his brand new baby cried, and his smile grew wider than ever.

The next afternoon Tashira went to the park to play. But the swings were still and the slides were empty because a gang of bad boys stood on the corner, scaring the little children away.

Then Officer Hamlette came walking along with his big, shiny badge. When the bad boys saw him coming, they ran away. Officer Hamlette stood on the corner with his arms folded across his chest, watching them go. And before long, all the little children came out to play.

"Thank you for being so brave, Officer Hamlette," called Tashira. "We were scared to play until you came."

"Oh, it's nothing," smiled Officer Hamlette. "It's just my turn to help, that's all."

He stood on the corner all day long, making the playground safe until the mothers called the children home to their suppers. And even when the sun went down, and the shadows faded into dusk, Officer Hamlette stood under a streetlight, keeping the neighborhood safe.

The very next morning, Tashira was riding her bike when she heard a small voice crying. She looked and saw black smoke pouring out of an open window!

"Someone needs help," she told herself.

She jumped off her bike and ran to the window. The smoke stung her eyes, and she wanted to turn away. But she glimpsed a little boy inside.

"I want my mommy," he sobbed.

"I'll take you to her," Tashira told him. She reached through the window and pulled him out.

"Keisha's still there," he cried, pointing to the house.

Tashira looked back through the window. The smoke was so thick now, she could not see inside.

"Wait right here," she said. "We need more help."

Tashira ran down the street. A moment later she was back with Officer Hamlette running beside her.

Officer Hamlette disappeared into the smoke. Tashira waited and waited. He was gone an awfully long time. When he finally burst out of the house, he had a little girl in his arms.

Now the big fire engines roared down the street with their sirens screaming. The firemen jumped off the trucks. They dashed into the house with long hoses.

The children's mother came running. "Oh, my babies!" she cried.

Revered Wilburn came running. "Tashira, you're a hero!" he shouted.

Tashira's teacher came running. "She's a hero!" she shouted. "Tashira's a hero!"

A big crowd gathered around. Tashira's own mother was there to give her a big hug, too.

"You're a hero, Tashira!" they all shouted.

Tashira just shook her head and smiled. "I'm not a hero," she said. "It was just my turn to help, that's all."

But everyone said she was a hero, all the same.

When Mother Reads Aloud

Children find heroes for life when mothers and fathers read, "Once upon a time . . ."

When Mother reads aloud, the past
Seems real as every day;
I hear the tramp of armies vast,
I see the spears and lances cast,
I join the thrilling fray.
Brave knights and ladies fair and proud
I meet when Mother reads aloud.

When Mother reads aloud, far lands
Seem very near and true;
I cross the desert's gleaming sands,
Or hunt the jungle's prowling bands,
Or sail the ocean blue.
Far heights, whose peaks the cold mists shroud,
I scale, when Mother reads aloud.

When Mother reads aloud, I long
For noble deeds to do—
To help the right, redress the wrong;
It seems so easy to be strong,
So simple to be true.
Oh, thick and fast the visions crowd
My eyes, when Mother reads aloud.

THE CHILDREN'S BOOK OF
AMERICA

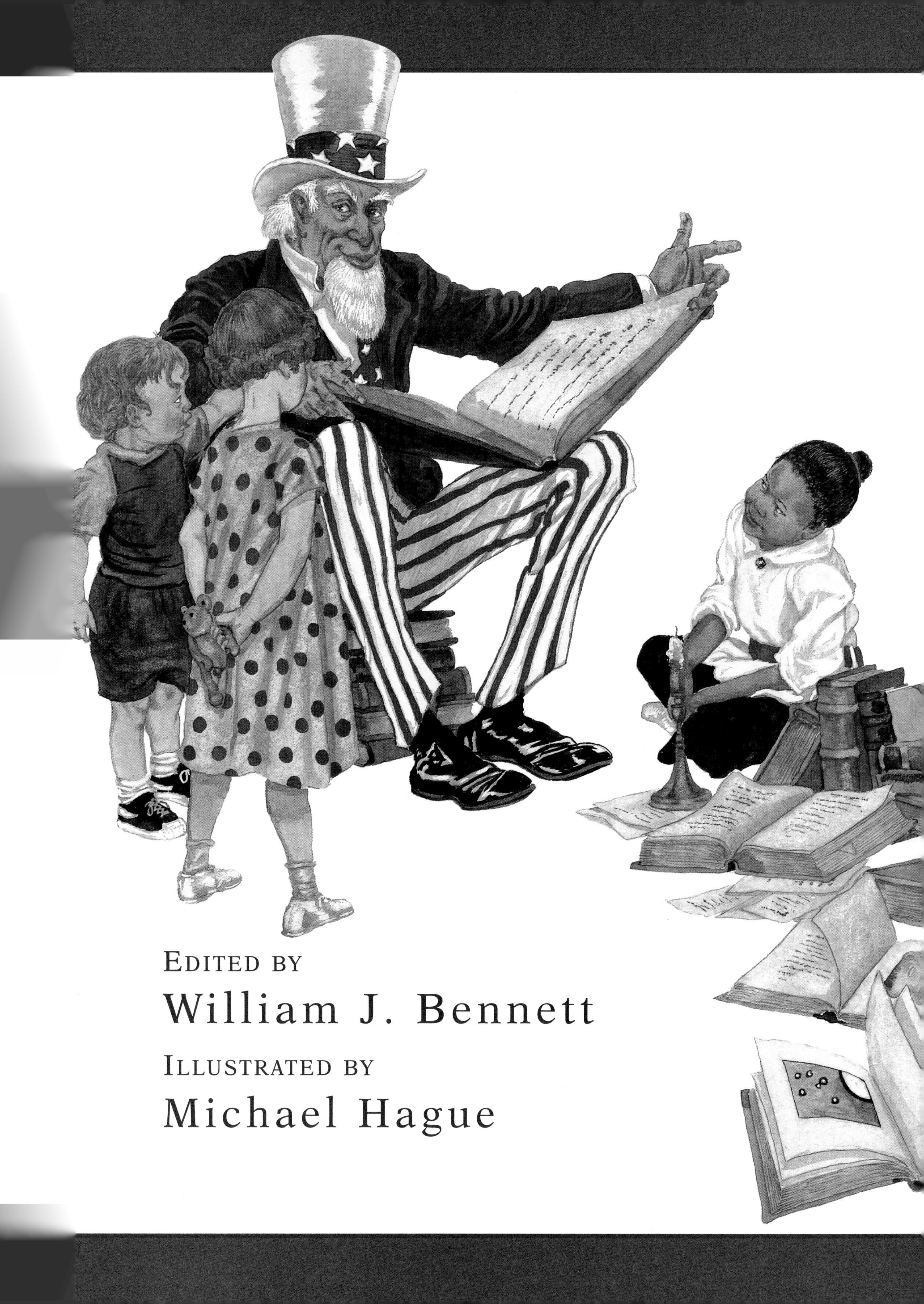
EDITED BY
William J. Bennett
ILLUSTRATED BY
Michael Hague

THE CHILDREN'S BOOK OF AMERICA

CONTENTS

To Dorothy and Clarence, Nancy, Lois and F. Robert, who taught Elayne and me to love our country
—W.J.B.

To Hopalong Cassidy
—M.H.

INTRODUCTION

Our Founding Fathers knew that a democracy flourishes only when its citizens cherish certain ideals and will not let them go. Love of liberty and equality. Faith in the Almighty. Attention to the cultivation of character. Respect for truth. Pride in good work. These are the kinds of principles that make America great, and if we are to stay great, we must raise our children to love them. Lessons about national character are taught in several ways: by the examples adults offer, by the expectations we set for youngsters, by the laws citizens obey, by the customs people honor. The spirit of America also comes alive for children in stories from our past. This book tells a handful of those stories with the aim of teaching young hearts and minds about some of our best ideals and aspirations.

In these pages, children meet some of the historical events, legends, songs, and poems that are their legacy. Abigail Adams, amid confusion and bloodshed, calmly takes up a pen to sustain her husband and their dream of independence. Lewis and Clark stand at the forks of the Missouri River and study its waters intently, knowing that somewhere upstream lies a nation's destiny. John Henry's hammer whirls like the wind and falls like a thunderclap, each stroke announcing that the American spirit *will* prevail. These episodes and images supply us with a sense of self as a nation, telling us who we are, where we come from, what we are about. They are part of what Abraham Lincoln called the "mystic cords of memory" that bind us together as a people.

When children hear of the Pilgrims at Plymouth, they learn about the love of freedom that led to this country's founding. In the story of our national anthem, they see that our forefathers had to stand fast in defense of liberty. In tales of the Civil War or the civil rights movement, they learn how long it took to extend that liberty to all Americans. When we share these stories with children, we teach them about the ideals we revere, the principles by which we want them to live. And thus we welcome them to a common American culture.

In introducing youngsters to their heritage, we should not hesitate to tell stories of heroes and heroines and thrilling adventure. Davy Crockett at the Alamo. Abe Lincoln splitting rails on the frontier. The world holding its breath while it waits for the words"The *Eagle* has landed." These stories ring with high drama and inspiration, and they win the hearts of children. Too often the modern day disposition is to take the heroism and poetry—the romance—out of our accounts of America. This shortchanges our young, because in truth the great story of America is filled to the brim with heart-stirring drama. As the historian Bernard DeVoto wrote:

> *If the mad, impossible voyage of Columbus or Cartier or La Salle or Coronado or John Ledyard is not romantic, if the stars did not dance in the sky when our Constitutional Convention met, if Atlantis has any landscape stranger or the other side of the moon any lights or colors or shapes more unearthly than the customary homespun of Lincoln and the morning coat of Jackson, well, I don't know what romance is. Ours is a story mad with the impossible, it is by chaos out of a dream, it began as dream and it has continued as dream down to the last headlines you read in a newspaper. . . . The simplest truth you can ever write about our history will be charged and surcharged with romanticism.*

If this collection conveys a sense of such grand adventure, it is in no small measure because of Michael Hague's own vision of that magical place called America. It was Michael who first suggested this book, and his brush, as always, beckons children into the stories. In these pages, it also opens their eyes to the beauty and goodness of this great country.

The story of America is, after all, a hopeful story. At times it has been faltering and uneven. But in the end, ours is a story of triumph. This really is, as the songs say, the land of the noble free, the place of the patriot dream that sees beyond the years, the home of heroes who, more than self, their country love. I hope this book helps us celebrate our unparalleled story. May it also help us share with our children the remarkable spirit of America.

"America the Beautiful"

—KATHARINE LEE BATES

A teacher named Katharine Lee Bates wrote this beautiful hymn in 1893 after seeing her country from atop snow-capped Pike's Peak in Colorado. She firmly believed that America's glory would last only as long as we crown its greatness with goodness, and its bounty with brotherhood.

O beautiful for spacious skies,
For amber waves of grain,
For purple mountain majesties
Above the fruited plain!
America! America!
God shed His grace on thee,
And crown thy good with brotherhood
From sea to shining sea!

O beautiful for Pilgrim feet,
Whose stern, impassioned stress
A thoroughfare for freedom beat
Across the wilderness!
America! America!
God mend thine every flaw,
Confirm thy soul in self-control,
Thy liberty in law!

O beautiful for heroes proved
In liberating strife,
Who more than self their country loved,
And mercy more than life!
America! America!
May God thy gold refine,
Till all success be nobleness
And every gain divine!

O beautiful for patriot dream
That sees beyond the years,
Thine alabaster cities gleam
Undimmed by human tears!
America! America!
God shed His grace on thee,
And crown thy good with brotherhood
From sea to shining sea!

The Legend of the Grand Canyon

Scientists say it took millions of years for the Colorado River to cut through a mile of rock and form the Grand Canyon. The Indians of the Southwest tell a different tale about the origins of this vast geological wonder.

In the dry, rugged country of the American West there once lived a great Indian chief. His wife was a wise and kind woman who filled his heart with happiness. They loved each other so deeply that anyone who saw them together could not help but smile. But one day the wife was bitten by a rattlesnake and departed this earth even before the sun went down.

The chief was a brave man, but he was not ready for this loss. Now there was no joy in his life, and he could do nothing but wander the land mourning for his wife. So deep was his sorrow that all of nature seemed to share it. The flowers bent their heads in despair. The stars dimmed in the sky. The birds left off their singing.

His people, too, felt his loss and grieved with him. No longer did they tend their crops or go hunting and fishing. Their fires sank low. They forgot their songs and dances. The village stood silent and sad.

When the Great Spirit saw the effects of so much sorrow, he sent his messenger to comfort the chief.

"Courage," the Spirit Messenger said. "Your wife is happy in the Land of the Spirits. When your work on earth is done, you will join her there. Until then, she wishes you to do your duty to your people, for they need your guidance, and are hard-pressed by your neglect."

"If my wife is truly happy, let me see her!" the chief pleaded. "If I can know she is at peace, I will be able to live without her until my own time has come."

Because there was still much work for this good man to do on earth, the messenger agreed to take him to the Land of the Spirits so that he could witness his wife's bliss.

The journey to the spirit world led across a savage terrain. The way was blocked by giant mesas that reached past the horizons and buttes that jutted into the sky. No human could scale such a wall. So the Great Spirit carved a wide, deep opening through the highlands and beckoned the chief to enter. At the bottom of this measureless chasm he found a narrow, winding trail, which he knew he was to follow.

The chief set out on the path, which no other mortal had tread. Around him towered the steep walls of the gorge. Sometimes they shone bright red in the sun; at other times they took soft purple hues or turned gray with the shadows of passing clouds. In places the cliffs vaulted so high they obscured the sky itself and shut out all light. Then the chief walked in darkness and lost track of the days and nights.

A long, long way he traveled. Many times, weary and footsore, he thought of turning back. But remembering his grief, he always pushed on. At last he came to the Land of the Spirits, and there he saw his lost love.

She smiled at him, and he saw that she was happy. Once again his own heart was filled with joy. As his grief departed, he remembered the people he had left behind. He saw the silent village, the dying fires, the withered crops. He knew his tribe needed his wisdom and guidance and that he should be at home.

Back through the deep canyon the chief hurried. Now the winding trail seemed not so long and rough, for he traveled with a new resolve. He knew that someday he would rejoin his wife. Until that time, he would strive to be worthy of her by doing his duty to his people. He returned to his village, where he ruled wisely and kindly the rest of his life.

But now the way to the Land of Spirits stood open so that people might go there whenever they pleased. Such was not the wish of the Great Spirit. For every mortal has work to do in this life and is called to that happy World Beyond only when his duties have been performed.

And so the Great Spirit sent a wild and thundering river to cover the footpath in the bottom of the gorge. To this day the river rushes across boulders and against sheer cliffs, hiding the trail so that no living beings may find the Land of the Spirits. But the mighty Grand Canyon itself remains, and all who see it are struck with awe.

The Pilgrims and the First Thanksgiving

America was founded by women and men who came to these shores lifting their eyes toward heaven.

In England four hundred years ago there lived a group of people we now call the Pilgrims. Their lives were not happy because they were not allowed to worship God the way they chose. When they tried to pray in their own way, they were thrown into prison or driven from their homes and jobs. Finally, in 1620, they could bear it no longer. Leaving all they loved behind, they boarded a small ship called the *Mayflower* and ventured out to sea. Perhaps they could practice their faith in that vast, far-off wilderness called America.

For two long hard months the Pilgrims crossed the stormy Atlantic Ocean. The *Mayflower* pitched and shook. Its beams groaned and its sides leaked. Men, women, and children grew ill. But at last they arrived in the New World. They came ashore, fell on their knees, and thanked God for bringing them across the wide and furious waters.

At once they began the business of founding their colony. First they built a large house for common use. Then they built smaller houses for each family. They named the village New Plymouth after the city in England from which they had set sail.

It was the heart of winter, and Plymouth Colony was in for a harsh, cruel beginning. The Pilgrims shivered in freezing winds and driving rains as they struggled to build their huts. The earth froze hard. Food was scarce—every night they wondered if there would be enough to eat the next day. And always they knew the Indians were watching. They heard their whoops and calls through the woods and saw smoke rising from their fires.

Then came the sickness. Many of the Pilgrims grew weak from lack of food and warmth. They lay in their beds, coughing and gasping for breath. Sometimes only a handful of settlers were well enough to cook and care for all the sick. Half the company died that long first winter. As the living buried their dead, they prayed and wondered if coming to America had not been a tragic mistake. But still they placed their faith in God.

Winter passed. The icy earth softened. One March day, as the settlers stared in wonder, a lone Indian strolled calmly into Plymouth, raised his hand, and cried "Welcome!" In broken English he told the Pilgrims his name was Samoset. He had learned their language from English fishermen who had visited the shores of the New World. He told them that the Indians who lived nearby were called the Wampanoags and were ruled by a wise chief named Massasoit.

A few days later Massasoit himself strode into Plymouth village with several of his braves. The Pilgrims spread a rug on the floor of an unfinished house and invited their visitors to sit. They ate and drank and talked together. They promised to live as neighbors and signed a treaty that kept peace between the two peoples for many years.

Massasoit brought with him an Indian named Squanto who spoke English. The settlers were amazed to hear this man's story. He had once been kidnapped by a sea captain and taken to Europe to be sold as a slave. Making his way to London, he had lived several years in the Pilgrims' own homeland before sailing back to the New World with English explorers.

It was Squanto who now stayed with the Pilgrims and helped them learn how to live in this strange, wild land. He showed them how to plant corn. He taught them how to

fish, and catch eels in the rivers, and dig in the mud for clams. He taught them how to hunt for deer in the forests. He showed them which berries were good to eat and which ones would make them sick. If not for Squanto's wisdom and aid, the little Plymouth colony may well have vanished.

Summer came. In the warm weather the Pilgrims grew stronger. With stout hearts they went to work in their fields and gardens. God blessed the land with sunshine and showers. The men and women of Plymouth watched the crops push up through the soil and prayed, for they knew they could not make it through the next winter without a good harvest.

The growing season passed and the days grew shorter. Fruit ripened. The pumpkins swelled orange and round. Autumn came in a blaze of glory, dressing the forests in gold and red and brown. The Pilgrims gathered the harvest, stored their food, and prepared themselves for the long, cold months that lay ahead.

They had much to be thankful for. The corn had grown well. The rivers and woods teemed with fish and game. The little houses were finished and ready for winter. The settlers had recovered their health and strength, and they had all good things in plenty.

It was time to celebrate the harvest and thank God for the blessings He had bestowed upon them. The Pilgrims sent a message to the Indians, inviting them to join a feast. Then they set about preparing. The men went into the fields and forests to hunt ducks, geese, and turkeys. The women stood beside the fires kneading, slicing, and roasting. The settlers set up long tables outside and placed rough benches beside them.

King Massasoit arrived with ninety of his braves. They brought five deer, their gift to the feast. Then the Pilgrims and Indians shared the bounty of the land. They ate fish and wildfowl and venison. From the bay there were clams, scallops, and oysters. From the forests came nuts and berries, and from the gardens came carrots, turnips, and onions. They feasted on stewed pumpkin, corn cakes, and bowls of chowder.

They celebrated with games as well. The settlers and Indians held shooting contests with both guns and bows. The young men challenged each other in foot races and wrestling matches. The Englishmen did jigs for the Indians, and the Indians in turn showed off their own dances.

For three days the feast continued. The Pilgrims knew well that more days of trial and hardship lay ahead. But for now, they rejoiced together over the gifts they had received. They thanked God for bringing them across the stormy ocean and seeing them through the long, harsh winter. They thanked Him for the bountiful fruits of their labor. They gave thanks for their Indian friends. And they gave thanks for this new land, where they could worship as they pleased.

Every year we remember that long-ago feast called the First Thanksgiving. On the fourth Thursday of each November, we rejoice that friends and loved ones have gathered safely together. We celebrate the fruits of our labor. We recall that throughout our nation's past, our ancestors risked their lives so we might be free. We bow our heads in thanks for all the bounty of this land and for the many blessings we have received.

Father Junipero Serra

In 1769, the king of Spain sent explorers from Mexico to California to begin settling that vast, beautiful land. One of their leaders was a priest named Father Junipero Serra. Often the settlers' efforts seemed doomed, but Father Serra refused to give up. Time and again in American history, such perseverance has made all the difference.

A line of men and beasts crept across the scorched California desert. Spanish soldiers wiped their brows. Mules staggered under bulky loads of supplies. Indian guides trudged wearily. They were looking for a bay called San Diego, but before them the earth lay brown and empty.

In the midst of this party limped a small priest in a gray robe named Padre Junipero Serra. He was born in Spain, but even as a boy he dreamed of exploring the New World. He came not to find gold or jewels but to spread the word of God.

Padre Serra's kind, bright eyes told of a gentle soul. They also spoke of a courage that never failed. "Always go forward and never turn back" was his motto.

The padre was not a young man. He had a sore left leg, which had been bitten by an insect years before and now

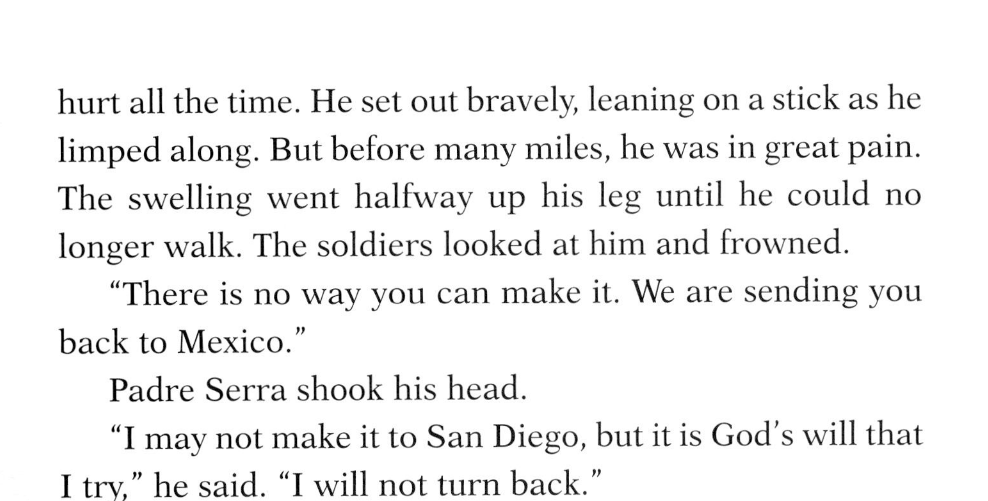

hurt all the time. He set out bravely, leaning on a stick as he limped along. But before many miles, he was in great pain. The swelling went halfway up his leg until he could no longer walk. The soldiers looked at him and frowned.

"There is no way you can make it. We are sending you back to Mexico."

Padre Serra shook his head.

"I may not make it to San Diego, but it is God's will that I try," he said. "I will not turn back."

That evening he sent for the young man who took care of the mules.

"Son, can you cure my leg?" he asked. The fellow was so surprised he could barely answer.

"But father, I only know how to treat the sores on the mules," he objected.

"Then pretend I am a mule." Padre Serra smiled.

The muleteer gathered the plants he needed, made a medicine, and spread it on the priest's leg. The next morning Padre Serra could walk again. The soldiers stared in amazement.

"This man lets nothing stand in his way," they whispered to each other.

The explorers hauled themselves across the barren land. They saw nothing but rocks, thorns, and sand. They labored up and down steep slopes. They pushed through cactus thickets. Their water supply ran low. Vultures circled overhead, watching and waiting.

The soldiers clutched at their dust-parched throats. They began to argue among themselves and talked of deserting.

"If we don't find water soon, we'll die," they muttered. "Better to turn back now, before it's too late."

"God is watching over us," Padre Serra told them. "We must never give up hope."

Sure enough, soon they came upon a beautiful stream. The desert gave way to more fertile lands, dotted here and there with clumps of trees.

At last they reached a place where the sea curved inland. Looking down on the wide blue bay, they spied two ships that had sailed north from Mexico to meet them. They had reached San Diego. With tears of joy they rushed to join their comrades.

But their happiness soon gave way to grim news. The ships had suffered a long, hard voyage. Many sailors had perished. More lay sick and dying. Their stores of food were running low.

The Spaniards held a council and chose a course of action. One of the ships, the *San Antonio,* would sail back to Mexico for more men and fresh supplies. The rest would try to hold on in California. The soldiers looked at one another uneasily. They knew the odds against them were growing day by day. The future looked dark.

Padre Serra put his fate in the hands of God and went straight to work. The settlers built a few crude huts where the sick could be nursed to health. One of the huts was set aside as a mission church. Padre Serra set up a cross facing the sea. From the branch of a tree he hung a bell. He called the Indians to come and hear about God.

But then followed months of hardship and disappointment. The Indians did not always come when Padre Junipero rang the mission bell. They did not know what to make of these newcomers and their strange ways. One day they attacked the mission. It broke Padre Serra's heart to see God's children fighting.

Sickness spread and more men died. Padre Junipero himself became ill. Almost all the food was gone. The men were always hungry and weak.

Every day the Spaniards looked to sea, hoping the *San Antonio* would return. But day after day there was no sign of aid. No word came from Mexico—only silence.

It seemed madness to stay any longer, and so a decision was made—they would pack up and go home. But Padre Serra begged his comrades to wait a while longer.

"In nine days it will be the Feast of Saint Joseph," he said. "Wait until then. If the *San Antonio* has not arrived, I, too, will admit defeat."

The padre's faith touched every heart. It was agreed to hang on a bit longer. Each day Padre Serra prayed, but each day the ocean lay empty. St. Joseph's Day arrived. The soldiers packed and prepared to go.

The afternoon shadows lengthened. The sun sank toward the sea.

"Have hope," Padre Serra whispered. "The day is not yet over."

The soldiers smiled at each other sadly. This man refused to give up!

Then someone pointed toward the water. A speck appeared on the horizon. The men held their breaths and watched.

"A sail! A sail!" The cry ran through the camp. It was the *San Antonio*, bringing men and food and medicine.

Was it a miracle? Those who watched Padre Serra fall to his knees and give thanks thought surely the good man's prayers had been answered.

The San Diego mission grew and flourished. It was only the first. Padre Serra and his comrades proceeded to found a string of missions along the California coast. At each one they hung a bell to chime the hour and summon all to prayer.

Some of the old missions still stand. When Americans hear the ringing of their bells, they remember the gentle little priest who limped hundreds of miles up and down California, telling of God and cheering others with these words: "Always go forward and never turn back."

The Bravery of Abigail Adams

The Revolutionary War years were a terrible and dangerous time. Many patriots had to flee their homes, and many lost everything they owned. Others suffered one of life's hardest challenges—they were torn from their loved ones. Abigail and John Adams spent many years apart during the period of our nation's founding, but their love for America and each other pulled them through.

The year was 1775, and sparks of rebellion whirled through the air. The American colonists were talking about freedom from England. British Redcoats swarmed through the streets of Boston. Patriots held secret meetings while men such as Paul Revere jumped on their horses and galloped from town to town, carrying news and warnings. Minutemen—farmers and tradesmen ready to fight on a moment's notice—shouldered their muskets and marched toward Boston. Everyone wondered if America and Britain were on the road to war.

In the village of Braintree, near Boston, Abigail Adams struggled amid the confusion and alarm. Her husband, John, was far away in Philadelphia at a meeting of the Continental Congress. There, leaders such as George Washington, Thomas Jefferson, and Benjamin Franklin were gathering to plot America's future. With John in Philadelphia, it was up to Abigail to care for the children and manage the farm alone.

There was much to do. The cows must be milked, the orchards tended, the accounts balanced. There were shirts to be sewn and pots to stir in the big kitchen fireplace. Many things were in short supply—sugar, pepper, pins—so Abigail did without them. Since the schools were closed because of the danger, the children were taught at home.

Minutemen, hungry and thirsty, tramped past the door, and Abigail gave them food and drink. Patriot families, fleeing Boston, poured into the countryside. Abigail spread blankets on the floor and gave shelter to as many as she could.

Abigail loved her husband and wanted him at her side in these unnerving times. But she also knew that America needed him for a while.

Almost every day she wrote to John, telling him about the children and the farm. She reported on the troubles in Boston and sent him her love and prayers.

"Good night. With thoughts of thee I close my eyes. Angels guard and protect thee."

All around her, Abigail could see and hear signs of danger. The countryside was filled with the sounds of men marching, drums beating, church bells ringing in alarm. Neighbors took sides against one another. Rumors spread like wildfire. There was news of bloodshed at Lexington and Concord, talk of fresh British troops sailing into Boston, warnings that the Redcoats were marching this way to arrest rebellious Patriots.

"In case of real danger," John wrote, "fly to the woods with our children."

Abigail responded bravely.

"Courage I know we have in abundance, conduct I hope we shall not want," she wrote, "but gunpowder—where shall we get a sufficient supply?"

Early one morning, before the sun rose, Abigail woke to a distant rumble. For a moment she lay still, listening for what she thought must be thunder. The deep booming came again, rolling across the hills from Boston. She leaped out of bed and dressed hastily by candlelight.

The noise woke her young son, Johnny, too. Taking him by the hand, Abigail climbed through orchards to the top of a nearby hill. They held their breaths and peered through the graying dawn.

Off toward Boston, smoke hung on the horizon. A faraway fiery glow filled the hazy air. Distant rockets burst in the sky and cannon blasts shattered the early morning stillness.

"What is it, Mother?" Johnny asked.

Abigail felt his eyes upon her, wide and uncertain, and she shuddered, for she knew it was the start of a long and terrible struggle for liberty—and that America's fate now hung in the balance.

Several days later in far-off Philadelphia, a gloomy John Adams sat in his boardinghouse room, his spirits sinking like a stone. He had just received a letter from Abigail telling of a terrible battle at Bunker Hill. Many brave men had fallen on both sides.

John was sick with worry about his family. Were they safe? Did they have enough food to eat? Where would they go if the Redcoats ran them out of their home?

He despaired at the slow work of the Continental Congress. There was so much squabbling among its members. How were the colonies to govern themselves? How could the rag-tag Patriot army stand up to the king's soldiers? Where would George Washington find enough men and muskets to fight?

Tired and lonely, John rose and paced the hot room. A frown creased his forehead. Perhaps the fight for liberty was a hopeless cause. Then his eyes fell on a few words in Abigail's letter.

> *"The race is not to the swift, nor the battle to the strong, but the God of Israel is he that giveth strength and power unto his people. Trust in him at all times. . . ."*

Tears of love and pride sprang to his eyes. He thought of his wife's courage and faith. Even as danger swirled all around her, she somehow carried on with the task of counseling her husband, protecting her family, and aiding the Patriot cause.

The clouds of doubt parted. With such bravery and devotion, nothing was impossible. John Adams knew the colonies could win their freedom. With fresh strength he picked up his pen and went back to the work of founding a new and great nation.

"Yankee Doodle"

The Spirit of '76 echoes in this song. British troops originally sang it to make fun of the shabby Colonial army, but the hard-fighting Americans liked the tune so much, they made it their own during the Revolutionary War. "Yankee" was a nickname for New Englanders, "doodle" meant a foolish fellow, and "macaroni" was slang for a dandy who liked to dress in style.

Yankee Doodle went to town,
A-ridin' on a pony,
Stuck a feather in his hat
And called it macaroni.

Chorus:
Yankee Doodle, keep it up,
Yankee Doodle Dandy,
Mind the music and the step
And with the girls be handy.

Father and I went down to camp
Along with Captain Gooding,
And there we saw the men and boys
As thick as hasty pudding.

And there was Captain Washington
Upon a slapping stallion,
A-giving orders to his men,
I guess there were a million.

And there I saw a wooden drum
With heads made out of leather,
They knocked upon it with some sticks
To call the folks together.

And then they'd fife away like fun
And play on cornstalk fiddles,
And some had ribbons red as blood
All bound around their middles.

Uncle Sam came there to change
Some pancakes and some onions
For 'lasses cakes to carry home
To give his wife and young ones.

But I can't tell you half I saw,
They kept up such a smother,
So I took my hat off, made a bow,
And scampered home to mother.

Westward with Lewis and Clark

The very first journey across our country and back took more than two years! Travel is faster these days, but blazing new trails is still the American way.

Two hundred years ago, most of this country was a wild, unexplored land that stretched toward the setting sun. Great rivers flowed out of the western frontiers, but where did they come from? There were rumors of rugged mountains, but how high did they reach? Somewhere beyond the mountains lay the Pacific Ocean. How far away was the sea? No one knew.

One morning in 1804, a clumsy-looking barge with a big square sail pushed up the wide Missouri River. Behind it came two long sturdy canoes called pirogues. All three boats were loaded with men and supplies. On the deck of the barge, two men stood talking. Their names were Captain Meriwether Lewis and Captain William Clark. They were setting out to do what no one had ever done before—travel across America to the great Pacific Ocean.

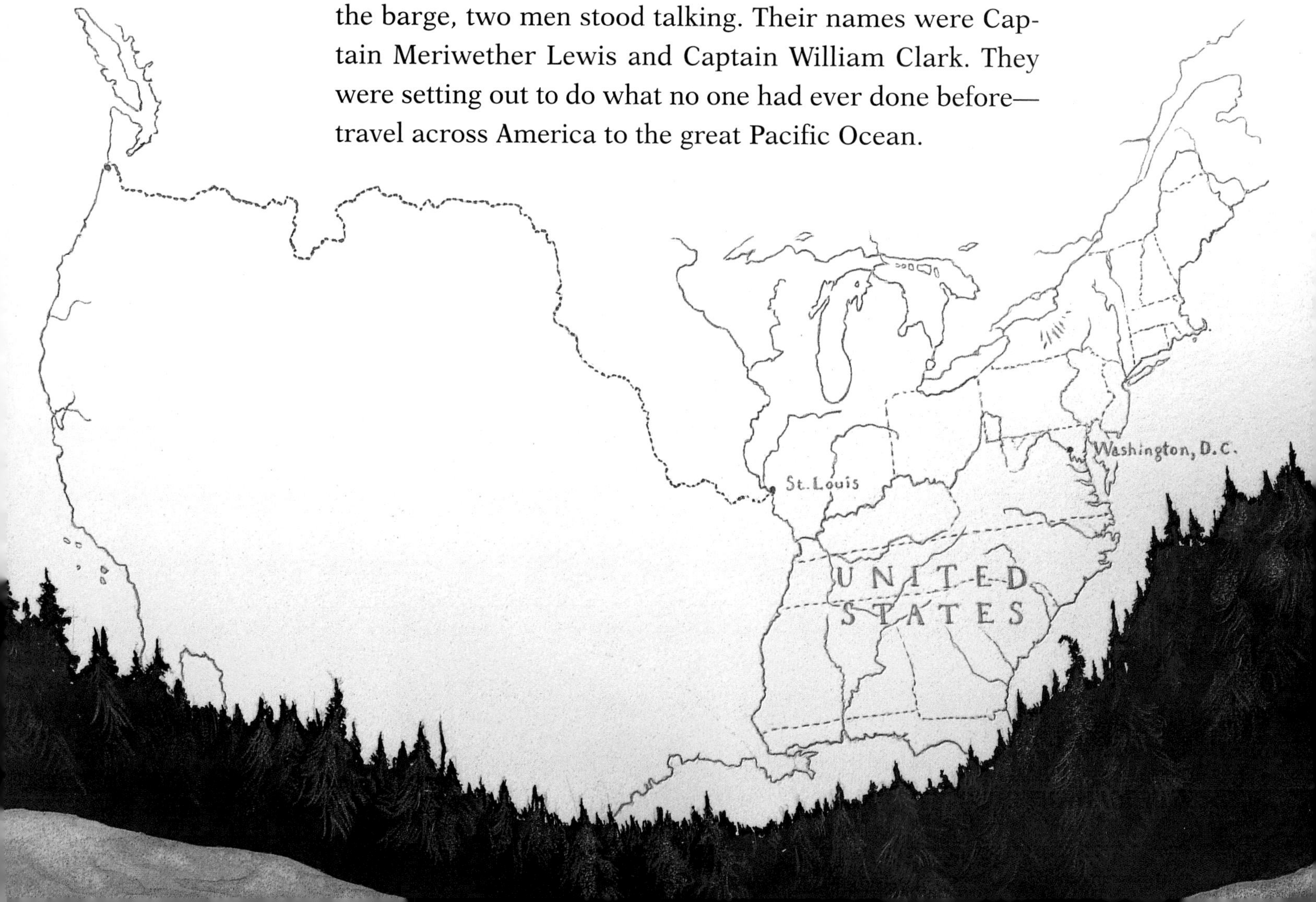

President Thomas Jefferson was sending this party to explore the boundless frontier. He wanted Lewis and Clark to find a path that would lead across the country. So this brave group of adventurers said goodbye to their friends and loved ones and started west into uncharted lands.

Progress up the Missouri River was hard and slow. Sometimes the explorers pushed the barge upstream with long poles. Sometimes they trudged along the riverbanks, towing the boat with a long rope. Captain Lewis and Captain Clark took turns scouting the land, collecting leaves, flowers, rocks, and even dinosaur bones to send back to Thomas Jefferson. They drew maps of their route so that others could someday follow.

The prairies stretched as far as the eye could see. The land teemed with deer, turkeys, and geese, which the explorers hunted for dinner. At night, the sky filled with blazing stars. Wolves howled. Bears rustled in the bushes. Sometimes, when the men rose in the gray dawn, they shook rattlesnakes from their blankets.

Soon they reached Indian territory, where tribes such as the Otoes, the Omahas, and the Sioux lived. Captain Lewis and Captain Clark held councils with the Indians. The proud chiefs came dressed in their finery—their skin painted yellow and red and green, their hair decorated with feathers and porcupine quills, their throats gleaming with bear-claw necklaces. Sometimes the Indians welcomed these newcomers as friends. Some tribes, however, feared that these strangers came to rob them of their lands. Always Lewis and Clark kept their eyes open and their guns within reach, ready for any surprise.

On the explorers pushed. Great plains spread before them, covered with herds of buffalo, elk, and antelope. Prairie dogs scampered into their holes. Beavers splashed by the river's shores. The land's size and bounty seemed to go on forever.

But now cold weather approached. Ice began to float down the river and the northern lights danced overhead at night. The tired explorers halted to build a winter camp. They crawled under buffalo blankets and snored while the blizzards piled snowdrifts all around their log cabins.

One day a French trader named Charbonneau arrived at the little outpost. Lewis and Clark decided to make him a part of their expedition since he spoke the Indians' language. With him came his young Shoshoni wife, Sacagawea, a name that meant "bird woman." That winter Sacagawea gave birth to a son, Jean Baptiste.

At last the snows melted and it was time to start out again. The big barge was loaded with everything the explorers had gathered so far—Indian clothes, animal skins, plants, insects, even live birds and a prairie dog—and sent back downstream to President Jefferson. The explorers, meanwhile, headed farther west. With the two pirogues and six new canoes they pushed upstream, into the unknown.

Sacagawea pushed steadily forward, too, carrying little Baptiste on a papoose board. It did not take her long to show her courage and quick thinking. One day a squall overturned one of the pirogues. The boat filled with water. Clothing, equipment, medicine, and all sorts of valuable instruments floated away. With her infant strapped to her back, Sacagawea plucked the supplies from the icy river. If they had been lost, the explorers might have been forced to turn back.

The land began to grow steep with hills. The men hauled the boats with tow ropes, wading waist-deep in the cold, swift water. High cliffs loomed over the river, worn into a thousand strange shapes like castles, columns, and towers.

They came to a place where the river forked into two large streams. Which way led to the mountains? The captains looked at the streams. In one, the water was muddy, but the other flowed clear over a bed of stones, like water coming out of highlands. They decided to follow this branch.

How would they know if they had chosen the right path? The Indians had said they would find a mighty waterfall on the river that led to the mountains. Tramping onward, the explorers came to a roaring wall of water. They were on the right track. They had reached the Great Falls of the Missouri.

The waterfalls were magnificent, but they were also a problem. The boats and everything else would have to be carried around them. The men cut down a cottonwood tree and made wagons to haul their supplies. Then the back-breaking work began. They pushed and pulled, dragging their cargo across the savage land. They caught at stones and bushes to haul the carts up the slopes. The prickly-pear cactus spines cut through their moccasins. Mosquitoes swarmed in the broiling heat. It took nearly a month to portage around the falls.

But now an even greater obstacle stood in their way—the snow-capped Rocky Mountains, vaulting toward the sky. Somehow they must get over these peaks.

Sacagawea pointed out landmarks she once knew as a child. Here, years ago, she had lived with her Shoshoni people. One day, without warning, an enemy tribe had swept into their valley. The warriors had seized little Sacagawea and carried her far away. Now, at last, she was returning home.

Soon the explorers found the Shoshoni and sat down to talk with Cameahwait, their chief. Sacagawea spoke as Lewis and Clark's interpreter. Suddenly, with a cry of delight, she jumped up and threw her arms around Cameahwait. She had discovered that he was her own brother!

Sacagawea told her people about Lewis and Clark's long journey. Chief Cameahwait agreed to sell them horses for the trip across the mountains. Two Indian guides would go along to show them the way. But they must hurry. Another winter would soon be upon them.

The explorers set out again. The hillsides were so steep that the horses kept slipping and falling. The brush was tangled and the men had to hack a trail as they pushed along. Rain, sleet, and snow fell. The food supply gave out, and the weary explorers began to go hungry. On and on they plunged through the snowdrifts, wondering if their journey would come to an awful end here in these high, craggy mountains. But at last they stumbled down onto a plain where some Indians gave them food.

With the mountains behind them, Captain Clark set the men about the task of making dugout canoes. Now the explorers would be able to ride the rivers to the ocean. Their goal was within reach.

Downstream they dashed on the great Columbia River. The boiling waters rushed through canyons and foamed over jagged boulders. More than once the boats turned over or crashed against hidden rocks. But at last the river widened and its current slowed. A white fog hung over its surface, and its waters began to move with the ebb and flow of the sea.

One morning the fog lifted. The weary voyagers stared ahead, barely able to believe their eyes. An endless expanse of water lay before them. They had reached the Pacific Ocean.

They had done it, crossing the vast stretches of land no one had dared to cross before. When Lewis and Clark found their way home again, more than two years after their departure, they brought word of a country richer and wider than anyone had dreamed. Towering mountains, endless plains, and fertile valleys were waiting. Now the path was open for the pioneers who would settle the nation from sea to sea. This brave group of men, and this one valiant Indian woman who traveled across a continent with her child on her back, had shown the way. They had shown just how big and great America was.

Paul Bunyan

Paul Bunyan reminds us that in America the sky—and our imaginations—is the limit. This is a land of big ideas, boundless energy, and mighty deeds.

Without a doubt, Paul Bunyan was the biggest, strongest, greatest lumberjack in history. No one knows for certain exactly how tall ol' Paul stood. But we do know that each morning he combed his big black beard with a pine tree to turn out any bobcats that had bedded down in his whiskers. When he swung his giant ax, he felled thirty trees at once and spawned tornadoes from Illinois to Oklahoma.

Most folks say Paul was born in Maine. (Some say he was born in five or six states all at once, he was so big.) He caused a lot of trouble as a baby, since every time he kicked or crawled around, he knocked down a few miles of fences, barns, and orchards. After a while the neighbors started complaining, so his parents built him a giant cradle and anchored it in the Atlantic Ocean. But every time he rocked in his cradle, the waves swamped two or three coastal towns. Once he fell overboard and caused a tidal wave. So his parents had to bring him back to port.

After that Mr. and Mrs. Bunyan decided to move to the wilderness, where Paul got plenty of practice knocking down trees as he was growing up. That's where he got the idea to invent logging. At first, he worked all by himself. But as word of his mighty feats spread and people heard about how he was clearing the wilderness to build the country, men started flocking from all over the world to lend a hand.

Before you knew it, Paul had hundreds of lumbermen working for him. He and his crew were always one step ahead of civilization, clearing the way for settlers and cutting the wood to build homes, churches, and schoolhouses. Before long, they'd cleared most of the forests in the East, and that part of the country was filling up with people. So Paul and his crew headed west to Wisconsin, where they set up camp.

Of course, cutting down trees works up an appetite, so the first thing Paul had to do was build a great big camp kitchen. The cookhouse was three miles long. The stove covered an acre of ground. It took a whole forest of firewood just to heat it up at sunrise. Seven lumbermen greased the griddle every morning by strapping slabs of bacon to their feet and skating across the sizzling surface.

Flapjacks, of course, are what lumbermen like best, so that's what Paul's cook, Sourdough Sam, made for breakfast. He made big flapjacks for the men and giant ones for Paul himself. As fast as he could cook them, three assistant chefs scooped them off the stove top with shovels and pitched them onto horse-drawn wagons for a mad dash to the mess hall. Wagons carrying the syrup sped right behind. (Paul dug the St. Lawrence River so that big barges of New England maple syrup could be floated to his camp.)

Paul kept the whole camp—kitchen, mess hall, bunkhouses and all—on a giant sled. When all the timber in a region was cut, he hitched Babe the Big Blue Ox to the sled and pulled the camp off to a new frontier. As Paul moved on, the farms and villages moved in behind him.

Paul had found Babe buried in a snowdrift during the Winter of the Blue Snow. (After all the snow had melted, Paul and his bookkeeper, Johnny Inkslinger, turned it into ink, so folks could write tales like the one you're reading now.) Babe was just a calf when Paul found him, but he was already pretty large, and he just kept growing and growing. He grew two feet every time Paul looked at him.

No one knows for sure exactly how big Babe grew to be, but old lumbermen swear he measured forty-seven ax handles between the eyes, and was heavier than the combined weight of all the fish that ever got away. Every time Babe needed to be shod, they had to dig a brand new Minnesota iron mine. Paul's blacksmith, Big Swede Ole, sank knee-deep in solid rock with every step when he carried Babe's shoes.

Of course, feeding Babe was a problem. He ate fifty bales of hay for a snack, and then it took six men to brush his teeth. Once his water trough sprang a leak, which is what started the Mississippi River flowing. After that, Paul dug the Great Lakes so Babe would have a watering hole.

Babe could pull just about anything you could hitch a chain to. Take, for example, the time he pulled the River That Ran Sideways into shape. The river was only twenty

miles long from north to south, but it had so many loops and bends and doubled back on itself so many times that it ran 212 miles from east to west. It took nearly two years to float logs downstream. That didn't suit Paul at all. Finally he spiked a chain to each bank, hitched Babe to the river, and yelled for him to pull. The big ox hunched his shoulders and gave a mighty yank. All the kinks came out, and after that the river was straight as a shotgun barrel.

Babe was a big help when the Winter of the Deep Snow came along, too. That was the winter it got so cold, the smoke coming out of the bunkhouse chimney froze in a column two miles high. Every morning one of the lumbermen had to climb up on the roof and chop it down. The boiling coffee froze so fast the ice got too hot to handle. It snowed and snowed and snowed till the tops of the trees got buried, and Paul's men couldn't find them to cut them down.

Finally Paul got an idea. He asked Ole the blacksmith to make a pair of giant, green-tinted glasses for Babe and turned him out to graze in the snowdrifts. When the Big Blue Ox saw the world colored green, he thought the hills were covered with clover and ate all the snow for lunch.

When Paul got through logging in Michigan, Minnesota, and thereabouts, he moved down the center of the country, through places like Nebraska and Kansas. He logged an awful lot of trees there and, while he was at it, cut down the hills for good measure. He leveled them flat as flapjacks so we'd have the Great Plains, and the farmers could plant miles of wheat for the growing nation.

Next, Paul and his crew logged the Southwest desert. That was the summer Babe got so thirsty, he drank all the water out of the Long Gone River and all the other rivers for miles and miles around. There's never been much water in the desert since then.

After he cleared the desert, Paul headed for the great Northwest, where he dug the Columbia River Gorge so that he could float his logs to the Pacific Ocean. But after a while even that corner of the country started filling up with people, making it hard for Paul to log on the kind of grand scale that suited him.

Some say he decided to hang up his ax. But most folks hold that Paul headed up to Alaska, where there's lots of untouched, wide open space left, and real frontier work to be done. There he strides across the mountains to log the frozen forests with Babe and treks up to the North Pole when he feels like stretching his legs a bit. Sometimes, just for fun, he breaks off huge hunks of ice and tosses them into the ocean for Babe to fetch, which is why the ships up there always have to be on the lookout for icebergs.

Wherever he is, you can be sure Paul is still busy. When you hear distant thunder rumbling, you know that's just the sound of him felling big trees, or moving mountains, or maybe laughing his deep, long laugh after a good day's labor. Wherever he is, you can bet your last dollar he's working hard, helping the country grow bigger and stronger.

The Story of "The Star Spangled Banner"

~ ADAPTED FROM EVA MARCH TAPPAN

The story behind our national anthem is a story of perseverance in defense of liberty. The battle at Fort McHenry that inspired the song took place during the War of 1812. In 1931, Congress chose "The Star Spangled Banner" as our national anthem.

The year 1814 found the people of Maryland in trouble. America was again at war with Great Britain, and a British fleet had sailed into the Chesapeake Bay. All along the shores, people fired alarms and lit signal fires to let their neighbors know danger was near. The ships sailed up the bay toward Baltimore. The bustling port was a rich prize. To take it, however, the British fleet would have to get past Fort McHenry, which guarded Baltimore's harbor.

As the warships crept upstream toward the fort, the crews could see a giant flag with fifteen white stars and fifteen red and white stripes flapping above the ramparts. It was the work of Baltimore flag-maker Mary Young Pickersgill and her thirteen-year-old daughter, Caroline. Their own house had not been large enough for the job of stitching together the enormous banner, so they had done some of the sewing in a nearby brewery where they could spread it across the wide floor. Now it flew as the proud symbol of an upstart country that was about to take on the most powerful nation in the world.

On the morning of September 13, the big British guns took aim at the flag and let loose a terrible fire. They shot huge bombshells that often blew up in midair. The attack lasted all day. When dark fell, the fleet used signal rockets, which traced fiery arcs across the night sky. It was a spectacular sight.

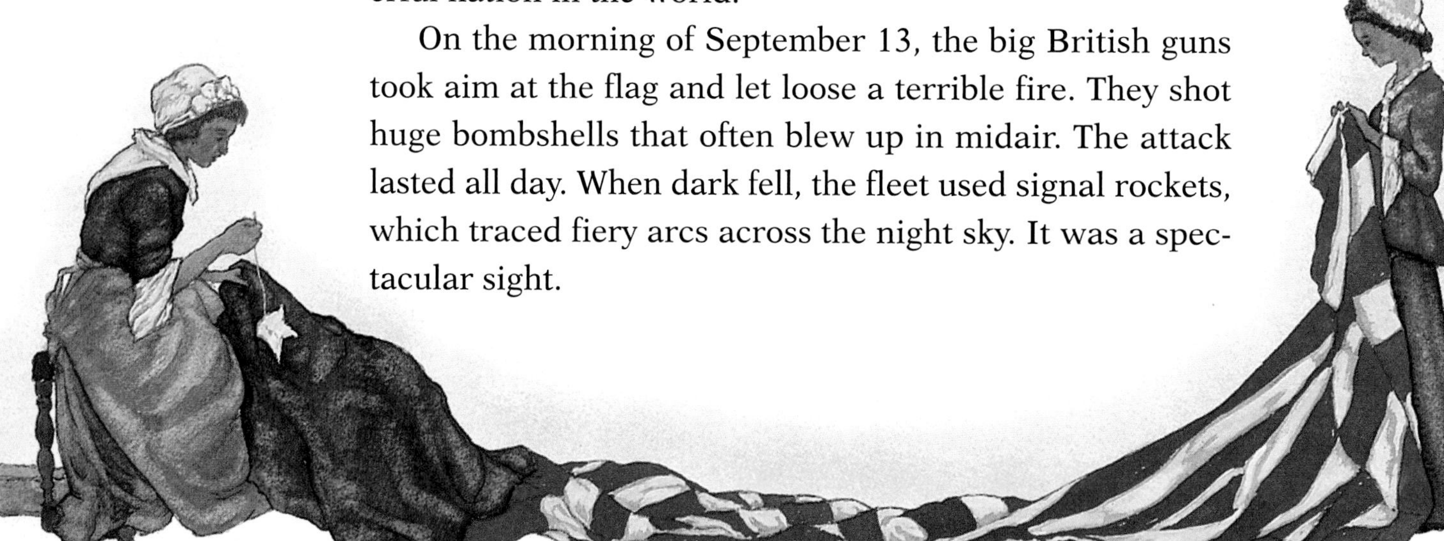

"If Fort McHenry can stand, the city is safe," Francis Scott Key muttered to himself. He stared anxiously through the smoke to see if the flag was still flying.

The young Washington lawyer was watching the battle from a little American vessel floating with the British ships. He had sailed out to the British fleet under a flag of truce before the fighting began. A friend had been seized prisoner by the British, and Key went to ask for his release. The British commander agreed, but he would not let Key return to Baltimore with any information he might have picked up. "Until the battle is over, you and your boat stay here," he ordered.

Key had no choice but to wait it out, pacing the deck and hoping the fort could hold out. The firing went on and on. As long as the daylight lasted, he could catch glimpses of the Stars and Stripes through the clouds of smoke. When night came, he could still see the banner now and then by the blaze of the cannon.

Finally, toward daybreak, the firing stopped. Key strained to see if the flag was still flying. "Could the fort have held out?" he wondered.

The faint gray of dawn crept into the sky. He could see that some flag was flying—but was it American or British? Who held Fort McHenry?

More and more eagerly he gazed. It grew lighter. A sudden breath of wind caught the banner and it floated out on

the breeze. This was no English flag; it was Mary Pickersgill's Stars and Stripes, still waving through the smoke and mist! Fort McHenry had stood, and the city was safe!

Overcome with joy, Key snatched an old letter from his pocket. Still watching the flag, he began scribbling a few lines on its back.

The British departed and the little American boat sailed back to the city. Key gave a copy of the poem he had just written to his brother-in-law, who had helped defend the fort. His brother-in-law sent it to a printer and had it struck off on some handbills. Before the ink was dry, the printer snatched one up and hurried to a tavern where many patriots were assembling.

"Listen to this!" he cried, and he read the verse to the crowd.

"Sing it! Sing it!" the whole company cried. Someone mounted a chair and sang the poem to an old tune. The song caught on at once. Halls, theaters, and houses soon rang with its strains as the British fleet disappeared over the horizon.

The years passed, and Francis Scott Key's words found a place in his fellow citizens' hearts. They became the anthem of a nation that stands always for freedom, just as the Stars and Stripes stood through that perilous fight so long ago.

"The Star Spangled Banner"

O say, can you see by the dawn's early light,
What so proudly we hailed at the twilight's last gleaming,
Whose broad stripes and bright stars, through the perilous fight
O'er the ramparts we watch'd were so gallantly streaming?
And the rockets' red glare, the bombs bursting in air,
Gave proof through the night that our flag was still there.
O say, does that Star Spangled Banner yet wave
O'er the land of the free and the home of the brave?

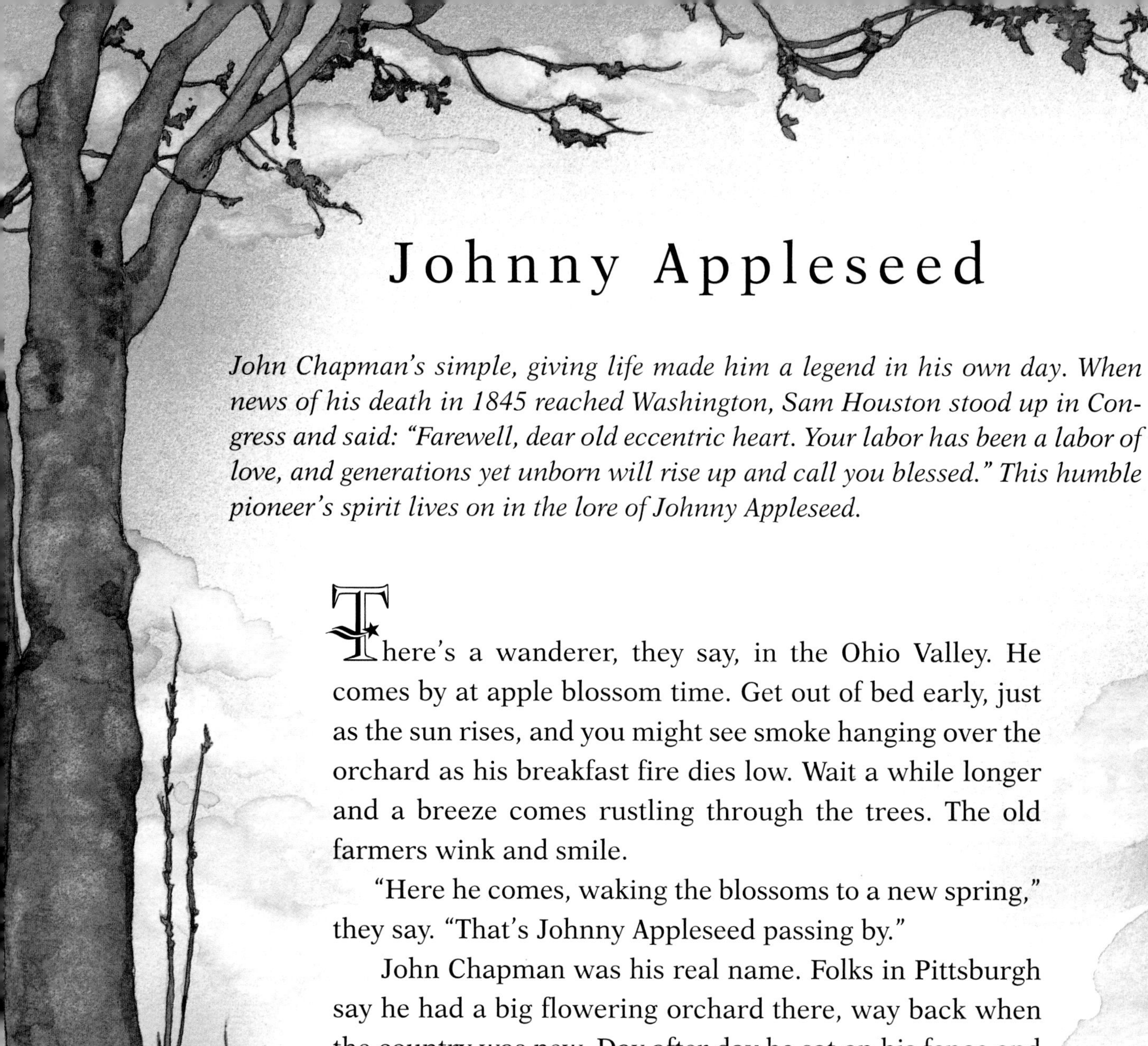

Johnny Appleseed

John Chapman's simple, giving life made him a legend in his own day. When news of his death in 1845 reached Washington, Sam Houston stood up in Congress and said: "Farewell, dear old eccentric heart. Your labor has been a labor of love, and generations yet unborn will rise up and call you blessed." This humble pioneer's spirit lives on in the lore of Johnny Appleseed.

There's a wanderer, they say, in the Ohio Valley. He comes by at apple blossom time. Get out of bed early, just as the sun rises, and you might see smoke hanging over the orchard as his breakfast fire dies low. Wait a while longer and a breeze comes rustling through the trees. The old farmers wink and smile.

"Here he comes, waking the blossoms to a new spring," they say. "That's Johnny Appleseed passing by."

John Chapman was his real name. Folks in Pittsburgh say he had a big flowering orchard there, way back when the country was new. Day after day he sat on his fence and watched covered wagons rolling by, full of pioneer families, headed west.

"Rough lives await them, full of hardship and toil," he thought. "What can I do to help?"

He watched the wagons go rumbling by and an idea took root in his mind. It grew and grew until it turned into a plan. So he filled a bag with apple seeds and slung it over his shoulder. Then he wandered away.

John walked through woods filled with oaks and hickories. He crossed fields where tall grasses waved in the wind.

Every once in a while, beside a stream or in a clearing, he would pause and untie his bag. With a pointed stick he dug holes, then stooped and planted some seeds. He covered them well, knowing they would grow in the sunshine and rain.

When the wagons came rolling west, the seedlings were green and strong. He dug them up carefully and gave them to pioneer families.

"Set them in the earth, and someday you'll harvest nature's jewels!" he told them. "Apples! Apple butter! Apple sauce! Apple cider! Jelly and pie!"

The settlers smiled and took the seedlings gladly. They planted orchards beside their new homes.

People began to call him Johnny Appleseed.

On he went. When his shoes wore out, he walked in his bare feet. Whenever he tore a hole in his shirt, he just took his needle and thread and sewed on a patch. For a hat he wore the old tin pot he used to cook his dinner.

"This is all I need," he would say. "God has made me rich, for I'm helping my fellow man."

Far and wide he traveled, across hills and valleys, through summer storms and winter snow. When night fell, he stretched out on a hillside. A mound of moss was his pillow, the starry sky his roof. When morning broke he would rise and walk on.

His orchards spread across the frontier, and so did Johnny Appleseed's fame.

Sometimes an Indian came striding along and walked with him through the wilds. But more often than not, he walked alone. Then, they say, the birds perched on his shoulder and deer ate from his hand. Sometimes he would pause and play with bear cubs while the mother bear looked on.

When a log cabin came into view, Johnny Appleseed was always welcome to rest his weary feet. Around the big fireplace the family would gather. The children lay on the floor, and Johnny would pull his Bible from his coffee sack shirt.

"Here's news straight from Heaven," he'd say. He would read of Noah's ark or the Sermon on the Mount.

His voice was so gentle and his smile so kind, they always asked him to stay awhile. He'd shake his head. "I've got work to do. Got to be on my way."

Ohio filled up with fences and barns and orchards.

"Time to be moving on," Johnny said. He headed west, planting seeds for the country as it moved west, too.

Some say he came to rest in Indiana, beneath the bough of an apple tree. Others say he just kept walking. Who knows how far he got? All across America—in the hills of Tennessee, the plains of Nebraska, the slopes of the Rockies, the wide valleys of California—people point to orchards and say: "Johnny Appleseed planted these trees."

Maybe he's been your way, too.

Abe Lincoln's School Days

"My best friend is the man who will lend me a book," young Abraham Lincoln used to say. The life of this backwoods boy still inspires our American faith that with enough hard work and study, any one of us can rise to the top.

Just about everyone who knew young Abe Lincoln remembered two things about him—his legs were forever getting longer, so his buckskin britches were always too short, and he always had a book in his hands.

Books weren't as plentiful as wildcats in the parts of Kentucky and Indiana where Abe grew up. But he read every one he could find. All the money he saved went to buy books, and he borrowed them from friends whenever he could. He once walked twenty miles just to borrow a book he wanted to read.

Abe walked to school, too, trudging hand-in-hand with his sister, Sarah, through forests where deer bounded, bears rustled, and squirrels chattered high overhead. The little log schoolhouse had just one room. The floor was dirt and the students sat on split-log benches. They learned their lessons by reciting them out loud, all at once. Some said their A-B-Cs, while others said their 1-2-3s. It was called a blab school because of the jumble of noise.

Abe learned to read, write, add, and subtract. The teacher taught manners, too, like how to say "Howdy do?" when you opened a door and walked into a room.

But frontier life was hard and left almost no time for sitting in class. There were always fields to be plowed, seeds to be planted, and rails to be split for fences. Abe used to joke that he went to school "by littles." He went a little bit when he was seven and a little bit more when he was eleven. He went a little when he was thirteen and went back a little while longer when he was fifteen. All together, he spent less than a year in school.

But what he tasted of books in class made him hunger for more. He would stuff a book into his shirt and go off to plow or hoe. When lunchtime came, he would sit in the shade of a tree and read. When he came home in the evening, he would go to the cupboard, snatch a piece of cornbread, take down a book, and read until his candle went out.

When Abe came across a passage that struck him, he copied it down so he could read it over and over again until he knew it by heart. If he didn't have paper, he wrote on a board, or a fence rail, or even the floor.

He did his arithmetic at night, too. He sat by the chimney and wrote numbers with charcoal on a wooden fire shovel, adding and subtracting by the light of the fire. When the shovel was covered with numbers, he shaved them off with a knife and started over.

Our future president liked to lie on his stomach beside the fire and read to sister Sarah. He read *Aesop's Fables, Pilgrim's Progress, Robinson Crusoe,* and *The Arabian Nights*. When he got a little older, he read the Declaration of Independence, and the U.S. Constitution. He wondered at the rich, mysterious phrases he found in the family Bible, too.

Once he borrowed a book about George Washington from a neighboring farmer. He read until he went to bed, then he put it on a little shelf where he thought it would be safe. But that night it stormed. The rain found its way into a crack between two logs in the wall and soaked the book through and through. It was almost ruined.

Abe felt very uneasy for the book was precious in his eyes, as well as in the eyes of its owner. He took the stained volume and set out for his neighbor's house.

"Well, Abe, what brings you here so early?" asked Mr. Crawford.

"I've got bad news," said a long-faced Abe.

"Bad news! What is it?"

"You know the book you lent me, *The Life of Washington*?"

"Yes, yes."

"Well, the rain spoiled it last night." He showed the book, wet to a pulp inside, and honestly explained how it happened.

"That's too bad, Abe," said his neighbor, stroking his chin.

"I don't have any money, Mr. Crawford," the young man said. "But I can work. I'll work on your farm till I've paid for the book."

Abe worked three days in his neighbor's cornfield until he'd made up for the loss.

"You've done a good job," Mr. Crawford said. "I guess you can keep the book."

Abe walked home that night with the book under his arm and a lesson lodged in his heart. He was sorry about what had happened but proud to have made amends and happy to have the book for his own, since George Washington was one of his heroes.

So he went on working and reading and growing. By small degrees he gained deep understanding. The boy who went to a one-room schoolhouse "by littles," who wrote on boards when he had no paper, who walked miles through the woods just to borrow a book, slowly became one of our country's wisest and greatest men.

"The Erie Canal"

Completed in 1825, before the age of the railroads, the Erie Canal was the nation's great water highway, connecting the Hudson River and Great Lakes. Boatmen sang this song as their plodding mules pulled barges between Albany and Buffalo, New York. Riders on canal boats might get a bump on the head if they failed to heed the mule driver's warning: "Low bridge, everybody down!"

I've got a mule, her name is Sal,
Fifteen miles on the Erie Canal.
She's a good old worker and a good old pal,
Fifteen miles on the Erie Canal.
We've hauled some barges in our day,
Filled with lumber, coal and hay,
And every inch of the way we know,
From Albany to Buffalo.

Chorus:
Low bridge, everybody down!
Low bridge, for we're going through a town!
And you'll always know your neighbor,
You'll always know your pal,
If you ever navigated on the Erie Canal.

We better get along on our way, old gal,
Fifteen miles on the Erie Canal.
'Cause you bet your life I'd never part with Sal,
Fifteen miles on the Erie Canal.
Git up there, mule, here comes a lock,
We'll make Rome 'bout six o'clock.
One more trip and back we'll go
Right back home to Buffalo.

Remember the Alamo!

Building this country took grit—sometimes the great courage to stand fast in the line of fire even when all hope was gone.

An alarm spread across Texas in early 1836. A great Mexican army led by General Santa Anna was marching from the south. In a few short days it would cross the Rio Grande River. Anyone who stood in its way would surely be destroyed.

In those times, Texas was part of Mexico. Santa Anna had seized power, made himself dictator, and demanded that all citizens submit to his rule. But the people of Texas refused. They made up their minds to fight for freedom.

The Texans hurried to arm themselves. Some gathered at an old mission once built by Spanish friars, a place called the Alamo. Here they would make their stand.

The Alamo was not much of a fortress. It was little more than a big stone building, a ruined chapel, and a large yard surrounded by a high wall. The men inside knew they would be outnumbered. But they would rather face a whole army than submit to Santa Anna's rule.

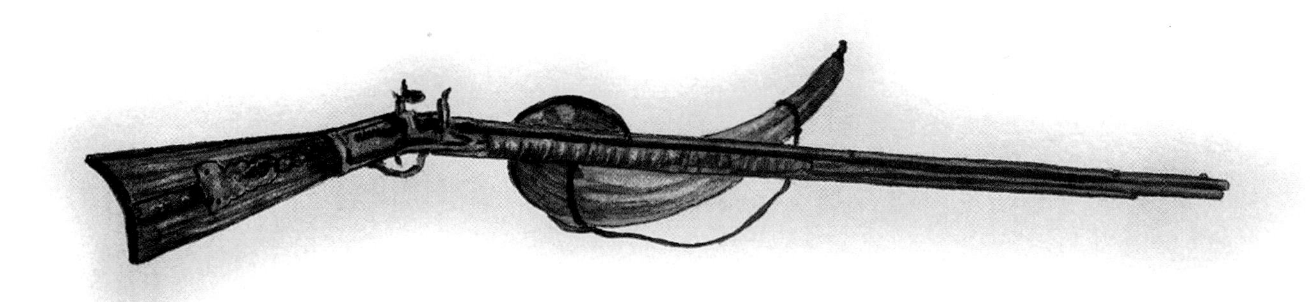

The defenders came from far and wide. There was young William Travis from South Carolina, the commander of the Alamo. There was Jim Bowie, who grew up among the blackwater swamps and tangled bayous of Louisiana. Bowie was famous for riding alligators and lassoing wild cattle, and even more famous for the way he handled his knife. Folks said that knife could tickle a fellow's ribs a long time without making him laugh.

Also at the Alamo was the great teller of tales and killer of bears Davy Crockett from Tennessee, in his coonskin cap and buckskin coat. Davy was already a legend. People said he could whip his weight in wildcats and grin a raccoon right out of a tree. With his long rifle, Betsy, he could shoot the wick out from under a candle flame.

Most of the men inside the Alamo were not famous, though. Most were not soldiers. They were ordinary men who had grown tough in lives of danger and hardship, men who had tamed the wilderness. They were fewer than 200 in number, but they had a love of liberty and knew how to stand up for themselves.

At last the Mexican army arrived. The church bells in town announced their presence. Santa Anna ordered a red flag raised atop the belfry. It meant: "Surrender or die. We will take no prisoners."

The Texans answered with a cannon shot. They would never give up.

Colonel Travis knew that to have a chance, he needed more men. He sent messengers bearing appeals for aid. "Our flag still waves proudly from the walls," he wrote. "I call on you in the name of liberty, of patriotism, and everything dear to the American character, to come to our aid with all dispatch. . . . If this call is neglected, I am determined to sustain myself as long as possible and die like a soldier who never forgets what is due to his own honor and that of his country. *Victory or death*."

The messengers departed and the men inside the Alamo waited. The Mexican army spread out around the fort and began to tighten its grip. Their cannon boomed, testing the strength of the old stone walls. In the lulls between the thundering fire, a strange sound floated on the smoke-filled air. It was music. Davy Crockett was fiddling inside the walls, raising the spirits of his comrades.

Days passed, and help finally came when thirty-two men slipped through the enemy lines and joined the force inside the Alamo. But that was all. The Texans now numbered 184 fighting men. Meanwhile, the Mexican army had been growing, too, swelling to 6,000 strong.

William Travis called his men together. He told them there would be no one else coming. If anyone wanted to try to escape, he would not hold him back. Now was the time to choose. He drew his sword and scratched a long line in the dust. All who wished to remain should step over the line.

They all crossed over, except one man. All but one elected to stand and fight.

The attack came early the next morning, before the sun rose. The cold, dark stillness was splintered by the blare of bugles, the crack of musket fire, and shouts of charging soldiers. They came from all four sides.

The Texas riflemen stood coolly atop the walls. Their deadly aim did its work. The first assault of the Mexican army wavered, broke, and fell back. The men inside the Alamo cheered.

The brave Mexicans rushed forward in a second charge. Once more the Texans drove them away.

But now came a third wave, and this time the Texans could not hold them back. The Mexican soldiers reached the fort, threw up their scaling ladders, and swarmed over the walls. In a few moments the battle was over. Not one of the Alamo's defenders was left alive. Colonel Travis, Jim Bowie, the great Davy Crockett—all were gone.

Santa Anna had taken the Alamo, but at a cost of hundreds of troops and a great delay. The stand-off at the Alamo gave other Texans time to rally their defenses. And it made them determined to fight even harder. "Remember the Alamo!" became the battle cry of the Texas army that soon met and broke Santa Anna's force.

The fight for independence was over. The dictator was defeated and Texans were free. Ten years later, in 1846, Texas became part of the United States.

To this day, we remember the story of the small band that stood unflinching against overwhelming odds, even to the last man. We honor their courage and devotion to liberty. And we recall that many brave Americans have laid down their lives in defense of freedom, whenever we hear the battle cry:

Remember the Alamo!

"I Hear America Singing"

— WALT WHITMAN

These lines are from Walt Whitman's book Leaves of Grass, *first published in 1855. Whitman was the poet of the common man. To him, the songs people sang as they toiled were among the most beautiful sounds on earth. The "varied carols" of Americans working hard still ring today, louder and stronger than ever.*

I hear America singing, the varied carols I hear.
Those of the mechanics, each one singing his as it should be,
blithe and strong,
The carpenter singing his as he measures his plank or beam,
The mason singing his as he makes ready for work, or
leaves off work,
The boatman singing what belongs to him in his boat,
the deckhand singing on the steamboat deck,
The shoemaker singing as he sits on his bench, the hatter
singing as he stands,
The woodcutter's song, the ploughboy's on his way in the
morning, or at the noon intermission, or at sundown,
The delicious singing of the mother, or of the young wife
at work, or of the girl sewing or washing
Each singing what belongs to him or her and to none else,
The day what belongs to the day—at night the part of
young fellows, robust, friendly,
Singing with open mouths their strong melodious songs.

The Tale of "Swing Low, Sweet Chariot"

Spirituals composed by unknown slaves rank among America's most beautiful music. As this story tells, it is wonderfully fitting that an ex-slave named Ella Sheppard grew up to help introduce "Swing Low, Sweet Chariot" and other spirituals to the world.

Sarah Hannah Sheppard stood beside the Cumberland River in Tennessee. In her arms she clutched her young child. Tears slid down her cheeks and her heart choked with grief. Sarah was a slave, and the day was fast coming when she would be sent away to a Mississippi plantation. Her mistress would not let her take the little girl with her.

She stared into the dark water and hugged Ella tighter. She could not bear the thought of losing her child. Better to jump into the swift, deep current and let the river carry them both away forever.

As she stumbled along the bank, an old woman rounded a curve in the road. She saw what Sarah was about to do and stretched out her hand.

“Don’t you do it, honey,” she called. “Wait a while and trust in the Lord. Let His sweet chariot swing low.”

Sarah stopped in surprise. The old woman came closer. She peered into little Ella’s face as if her aged eyes could see a long way.

“There is great work for this child to do here on earth,” she said softly. “She’s going to stand before kings and queens. So don’t you do it, honey. Just you wait. The Lord’s going to carry the both of you home.”

Sarah nodded and stepped away from the bank. Holding Ella close, she turned and slowly walked home. Before long she was parted from her precious child. But still she trusted in God.

The wise old woman’s prophecy came true. Little Ella grew up strong and beautiful, and her heart was full of music. After the Civil War, when slavery was no more, she enrolled in Fisk University in Nashville, Tennessee. There she played the piano with the Fisk Jubilee Singers. They lifted their voices with the old songs, the tunes their parents and grandparents had sung when they were slaves, asking God to set them free. The land rang with the deep, stirring spirituals. Ella Sheppard and the Jubilee Singers traveled far and wide—even across the sea to Europe, where they sang before dukes, princes, and queens.

But Ella did not forget her mother. Searching and searching, at last she found Sarah. She brought her home to take care of her always. And often the loving daughter sang this old, sweet song, which she had helped to spread throughout the world.

“Swing Low, Sweet Chariot”

Swing low, sweet chariot,
Coming for to carry me home.
Swing low, sweet chariot,
Coming for to carry me home.

I looked over Jordan and what did I see,
Coming for to carry me home?
A band of angels coming after me,
Coming for to carry me home.

If you get there before I do,
Coming for to carry me home,
Tell all my friends I'm coming too,
Coming for to carry me home.

Sometimes I'm up and sometimes I'm
down,
Coming for to carry me home,
But still my soul seems heavenly bound,
Coming for to carry me home.

Swing low, sweet chariot,
Coming for to carry me home.
Swing low, sweet chariot,
Coming for to carry me home.

Robert E. Lee and the Wounded Soldier

This incident happened during the Civil War, the awful struggle that divided America against itself. In the actions of a defeated Confederate general, we see the kind of honest compassion that, in Lincoln's words, helped bind up the nation's wounds.

A fierce battle had just ended at Gettysburg, Pennsylvania, the fiercest battle of the Civil War. The Union army had won a great victory, and the defeated Confederate forces were now retreating from the field.

A Union soldier lay on the ground not far from Cemetery Ridge, his leg shattered by a bullet. He hated slavery and had grown to hate Southerners during the war. He had fought them bitterly and could see nothing good in any of them. Now his pain made him hate them even more.

The stricken man saw a group of Confederate officers riding along. At their front rode a man with a straight back and snow-white beard. The soldier knew at once it was General Robert E. Lee, the enemy's leader. Anger swelled in his breast.

Though faint from fever and loss of blood, he raised his hands, looked Lee in the face, and shouted as loud as he could: "Hurrah for the Union!"

General Lee heard the mocking cry. He looked, stopped his horse, and dismounted. Slowly he walked toward the wounded man. The Union soldier shrank back, certain the Rebel general intended to kill him.

But Lee looked down with such a sad expression that at once all fear left the wounded man. He wondered what the Confederate general meant to do.

General Lee reached out and grasped the soldier's hand firmly. Looking into his eyes, he said softly, "My son, I hope you will soon be well."

The Union soldier stared back. The expression on General Lee's face was so weary and kind that he knew he would never forget it if he lived a thousand years. There he was, beaten, retiring from a field that had cost him and his army their last hope, and yet he stopped to comfort a wounded foe who had taunted him as he passed by!

General Lee rode slowly away. His words, however, lodged in the soldier's heart and stayed there long after the war ended.

Margaret of New Orleans

— Adapted from Sarah Cone Bryant

Throughout our history, countless people have come to this land of opportunity and receiving much, have given even more in return. Margaret Haughery was one such immigrant. Her life, modest and compelling, is a reminder that charity is among our most honored national traits.

If you ever go to beautiful New Orleans, someone might take you down to the old part of the city along the wide Mississippi River and show you a statue that stands there. It depicts a woman sitting in a low chair, with her arms around a child who leans against her. The woman is not very pretty. She wears thick shoes and a plain dress. She is stout and short, and her face is square-chinned. But her eyes look at you like your mother's.

This is the statue of a woman named Margaret. Her whole name was Margaret Haughery, but no one in New Orleans remembers her by it, any more than you would think of your sister or your best friend by her full name. She is just Margaret. Born across the ocean in Ireland more than 150 years ago, she came to America when she was just a little girl and grew up here. Her statue is one of the first ever made in our country in honor of a woman.

As a young woman Margaret was all alone in the world. She was poor but strong, and she knew how to work. All day, from morning until evening, she ironed clothes in a laundry. And every day, as she worked by the window, she saw the little children from the nearby orphanage working and playing. They had no mothers or fathers of their own to take care of them. Margaret knew they needed a good friend.

You would hardly think that a poor woman who worked in a laundry could be much of a friend to so many children. But Margaret was. She went straight to the kind Sisters who ran the orphanage and told them she wanted to help the little ones.

So she gave part of her wages every week to the orphanage. She worked so hard that she was able to save some money, too. With this, she bought two cows and a delivery cart. She carried milk to her customers in the little cart every morning. As she went along, she asked for leftover food from hotels and rich houses, and brought it back in the cart to the hungry children in the orphanage. In the very hardest times, that was often all the food the children had.

In spite of her giving, Margaret was so careful and so good at business that she was able to buy more cows and earn more money. With this, she helped build a home for orphan babies. She called it her baby house.

After a time, Margaret had a chance to take over a bakery, and then she became a bread woman instead of a milk woman. She carried the bread just as she had carried the milk, in her cart. And still she kept giving money to the orphanage.

Then a great war came, the Civil War. In all the trouble and fear of that time, Margaret drove her cart. Somehow she always had enough bread to give to the hungry soldiers and to her babies, besides what she sold. And despite all this, she earned enough so that when the war was over she built a big steam factory to make her bread.

By this time everybody in the city knew her. The children all over New Orleans loved her. The businessmen were proud of her. The poor people all came to her for advice. She used to sit at the open door of her office in a calico gown and a little shawl and give a good word to everybody, rich or poor.

Margaret grew old and, by and by, one day she died. When it was time to read her will, people found that, even with all her giving, she had still saved a great deal of money—and she had left every cent of it to the orphanages of the city. Each one of them was given something. Whether the children were boys or girls, white or black, Jews or Christians, made no difference, for Margaret always said, "They are all orphans alike." Her splendid will was signed with an *X* instead of a name, for Margaret had never learned to read or write.

The people of New Orleans said, "She was a mother to the motherless. She was a friend to those who had no friends. She had wisdom greater than schools can teach. We will not let her memory go from us." So they made a statue of her, just as she used to look sitting in her office door or driving in her own little cart. And there it stands today, in memory of the great love and the great power of plain Margaret Haughery of New Orleans.

MARGARET

“Home on the Range”

This song has been called the cowboy’s national anthem. Here is the America of wide-open spaces and boundless optimism—the land where seldom is heard a discouraging word.

Oh, give me a home where the buffalo roam,
Where the deer and the antelope play,
Where seldom is heard a discouraging word,
And the skies are not cloudy all day.

Chorus:
Home, home on the range,
Where the deer and the antelope play,
Where seldom is heard a discouraging word,
And the skies are not cloudy all day.

Where the air is so pure, the zephyrs so free,
The breezes so balmy and light,
That I would not exchange my home on the range
For all the cities so bright.

How often at night when the heavens are bright
With the light of the glittering stars,
Have I stood here amazed and asked as I gazed
If their glory exceeds that of ours.

Oh, give me a land where the bright diamond sand
Flows leisurely down the stream,
Where the graceful white swan goes gliding along
Like a maid in a heavenly dream.

John Henry and the Steam Drill

Some say this race between man and machine really took place in the 1870s in West Virginia, although no one can say for sure. But the story and ballad of John Henry remind us of a great American tradition: pride and pleasure in work.

Folks say John Henry was born to be a steel-driving man. His twelve-pound hammer whirled round his shoulders like the wind. When it fell, it crashed like a thunderclap. When it hit steel, sparks rained like lightning.

John Henry lived in the days when something mighty big was happening in America. From coast to coast, men were building railroads—great railroads like the Union Pacific, the Illinois Central, and the Chesapeake and Ohio. John Henry helped lay the tracks. Sometimes he drove big steel spikes into the cross-ties to hold the rails in place. Other times he hammered long steel drills into rock to cut tunnels through the mountains. After he drilled a hole, the blasting crews packed it with dynamite, lit a fuse, and blew the rock to pieces.

This story takes place when the C&O Railroad was digging the Big Bend Tunnel through the high Appalachian Mountains in West Virginia. John Henry was there, driving steel faster and harder than any five men working together. His big hammer arced through the air like a rainbow. It rang like silver and shone like gold. It pealed like a hundred bells the day Captain Tommy walked up and laid a hand on John Henry's shoulder.

"John Henry," he said, "there's a man outside selling a shiny, new steam drilling machine. Says it can do the work of six men. But I say you can beat the steam drill. What do you say?"

John Henry lowered his hammer.

"Captain," he said, "I'd rather die than let that machine beat me down."

John Henry told his captain,
"A man ain't nothin' but a man,
Fo' I let that steam drill beat me down
I'll die with this hammer in my hand, Lord, Lord,
I'll die with this hammer in my hand."

And every man in that tunnel cheered.

The contest started the very next morning. The big steam drill stood on the left, gleaming and hissing and humming. John Henry stood on the right with a big twenty-pound hammer in his hand. A crowd swarmed all around.

Captain Tommy blew his whistle and the race was on.

The steam drill gave a shriek and a roar. It smashed into the mountain, gnawing rock and spitting clouds of dust.

John Henry swung his hammer with giant mountain-cracking strokes. The drill head smoked from the force of his blows. Men stood around with buckets of water to pour, trying to keep the hammer from catching fire.

After a while John Henry paused to catch his breath. He glanced at Little Bill, who held the long steel drill in place.

"How we doing, Little Bill?" he asked.

Little Bill shook his head. A frown creased his dusty brow.

"Machine's ahead, John Henry."

John Henry just laughed and swung harder. The sparks flew high as steel struck steel. His hammer burned like a torch, and the whole tunnel glowed with the flame.

"How we doing now?" John Henry yelled.

Little Bill grinned.

"Steam drill broke down," he said. "They'll have to drag it outside and fix it. Now's the time to catch up."

John Henry laughed again and drove harder.

John Henry told his captain,
"Look yonder, what do I see?
That drill's done broke, and the hole's done choke,
And it can't drive steel like me, Lord, Lord,
It can't drive steel like me."

But pretty soon the steam drill was chugging and hissing again, tearing away at the rock. John Henry was driving steel, too. His hammer streaked like a meteor. The mountain rumbled with every stroke. And John Henry's heart pounded against his ribs so hard, folks say you could hear them crack.

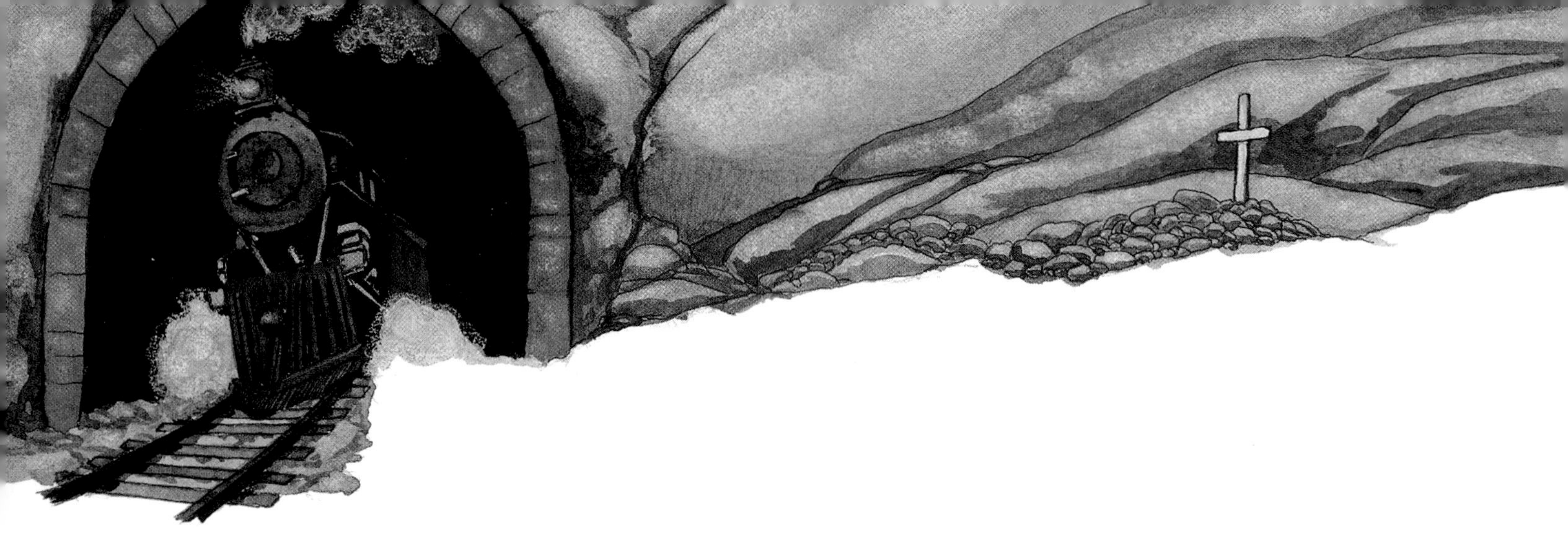

"Time!" Captain Tommy yelled. The race was over. The judges measured the holes. John Henry had driven fifteen feet into the rock. The steam drill had gone only nine.

The crowd roared and rushed forward. But John Henry slumped against his hammer. The next minute he was on the ground.

"I beat that steam engine," he gasped, "but I broke inside."

John Henry was hammerin' in the mountain,
Till the handle of his hammer caught fire,
He drove so hard that he broke his poor heart,
Then he laid down his hammer and he died,
Lord, Lord,
He laid down his hammer and he died.

They carried him outside and laid him to rest near the mouth of the tunnel with his hammer in his hand. Before long, the big new machines took over the work of the steel-driving men. But the men never stopped singing about how John Henry whipped that steam drill. And they say that if he were alive today, he'd beat any other machine that came along, too.

They took John Henry to the tunnel,
And they buried him in the sand,
An' every locomotive come rollin' by
Says, "There lies a steel-drivin' man, Lord, Lord,
There lies a steel-drivin' man."

"The New Colossus"

— Emma Lazarus

Poet and patriot Emma Lazarus worked tirelessly to aid the thousands of Jewish refugees who flocked to America in the 1880s after suffering terrible persecution in Russia. Years later, her now-famous poem was engraved on the base of the Statue of Liberty. Its title refers to the Colossus of Rhodes, one of the seven wonders of the ancient world, a giant bronze statue that overlooked the Greek city's harbor. These verses remind us that America is the world's brightest beacon of freedom and hope.

Not like the brazen giant of Greek fame,
With conquering limbs astride from land to land;
Here at our sea-washed, sunset gates shall stand
A mighty woman with a torch, whose flame
Is the imprisoned lightning, and her name
Mother of Exiles. From her beacon-hand
Glows world-wide welcome; her mild eyes command
The air-bridged harbor that twin cities frame.

"Keep, ancient lands, your storied pomp!" cries she
With silent lips. "Give me your tired, your poor,
Your huddled masses yearning to breathe free,
The wretched refuse of your teeming shore,
Send these, the homeless, tempest-tost to me:
I lift my lamp beside the golden door."

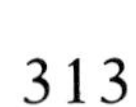

The Wizard of Menlo Park

One night in 1914 an awful fire roared through one of Thomas Edison's factories in West Orange, New Jersey. By morning all seemed lost. "We've just cleared out a bunch of old rubbish," Edison insisted. "We'll build it back bigger and better." That sort of can-do attitude made Edison an ingenious inventor. And it has made American invention and industry the greatest in the world.

Thomas Alva Edison was a curious boy. He was always poking and prodding to find out how things worked and asking all sorts of questions. Why is the sky blue? Why does the wind blow? Why do bees buzz?

"Why shouldn't people be able to fly like birds?" he asked himself. So he set about trying to figure out a way.

Thomas's laboratory was in the basement of the Edison house in Port Huron, Michigan. There he collected old jars, wires, chemicals, and scraps of metal to perform his experiments. His eye lit upon a bottle of Seidlitz powder, a popular medicine in those days. Mix a little powder in a glass of water and you got lots of dancing bubbles.

"All you have to do is fill your stomach with these bubbles and you'll float like a balloon," Thomas thought. That was it!

As good as the idea was, Thomas was not about to try it on himself. So now he needed a volunteer for his experiment. In the backyard he found his friend Michael Oates. Thomas carefully explained his plan.

"Fly? Who wants to fly?" Michael frowned. "Besides, how am I gonna get down?"

Thomas had already thought of that.

"Just grab hold of those tree branches as you go floating by," he instructed. "I'll run and get a ladder and haul you back to earth."

Michael was willing. He took a deep breath, threw his head back, and gulped down a big dose.

The two boys stood blinking and waiting.

"Flap your arms!" Thomas yelled.

Michael flapped.

"Jump!"

Michael was looking a little light-headed. He wobbled. He hiccuped.

He dropped like a stone.

Michael Oates got a stomachache. Thomas got a switching.

But he never gave up asking questions and trying to find answers. When he grew up, he built a laboratory in Menlo Park, New Jersey, and brought together a team of swift-minded men to help him in his experiments. It was the world's very first "invention factory"—a business devoted to dreaming up and testing useful devices.

Before long he invented a machine that made him famous all over the world. He drew a sketch of his idea on a piece of paper and gave it to the men in the lab to make. They shook their heads in doubt but carefully built the machine and brought it to his desk. As they crowded around, he turned the machine's crank and shouted a nursery rhyme: "Mary had a little lamb. Its fleece was white as snow. . . ."

Then he turned the crank again, and all the men jumped back when they heard the same voice coming out of the machine: "Mary had a little lamb. . . ."

Thomas Edison had invented the phonograph. For the very first time, the world could record and play back sounds.

Most of his inventions did not come so quickly, though. Almost always he had to try and try again. One time he conducted experiment after experiment without finding the answer he needed. A friend said he was sorry the tests were failing.

"We haven't failed." Edison smiled. "Now we know a thousand things that won't work, so we're that much closer to finding what will."

His most important invention came that way—by trying again and again. In those days, homes were lit by candles or gas lamps. But Edison knew there must be a way to make a better source of light. He spent a year testing and searching. He tried experiment after experiment. Then one day he ran an electric current through a thin thread of baked cotton inside a glass bulb. The lamp gleamed one hour, then two—then into the night. Thomas stayed up until sunrise, watching the little lightbulb glow. He knew the world would change forever after that night. The age of electric light had dawned.

Soon people began calling Thomas Edison the Wizard of Menlo Park.

Thomas just laughed. Wizard? No, it was just plain hard work that led to such marvelous inventions. "Genius is one percent inspiration and ninety-nine percent perspiration," he said.

Edison spent many more years improving his lightbulb and thinking of ways to carry electricity to lamps in homes, offices, factories, and streets. Over the course of his life he came up with more than 1,000 inventions. He created different kinds of batteries, methods to manufacture chemicals, and a way to make the telephone better. He even invented a machine to show moving pictures, thereby helping to found one of America's most famous industries: the movies.

Thomas Edison went on working, testing, and inventing all his life. Even as an old man, he kept searching for answers to his questions. "I am long on ideas, but short on time," he said. When he died in 1931 at the age of eighty-four, lights were dimmed all across the country to honor the Wizard of Menlo Park, the greatest of all American inventors.

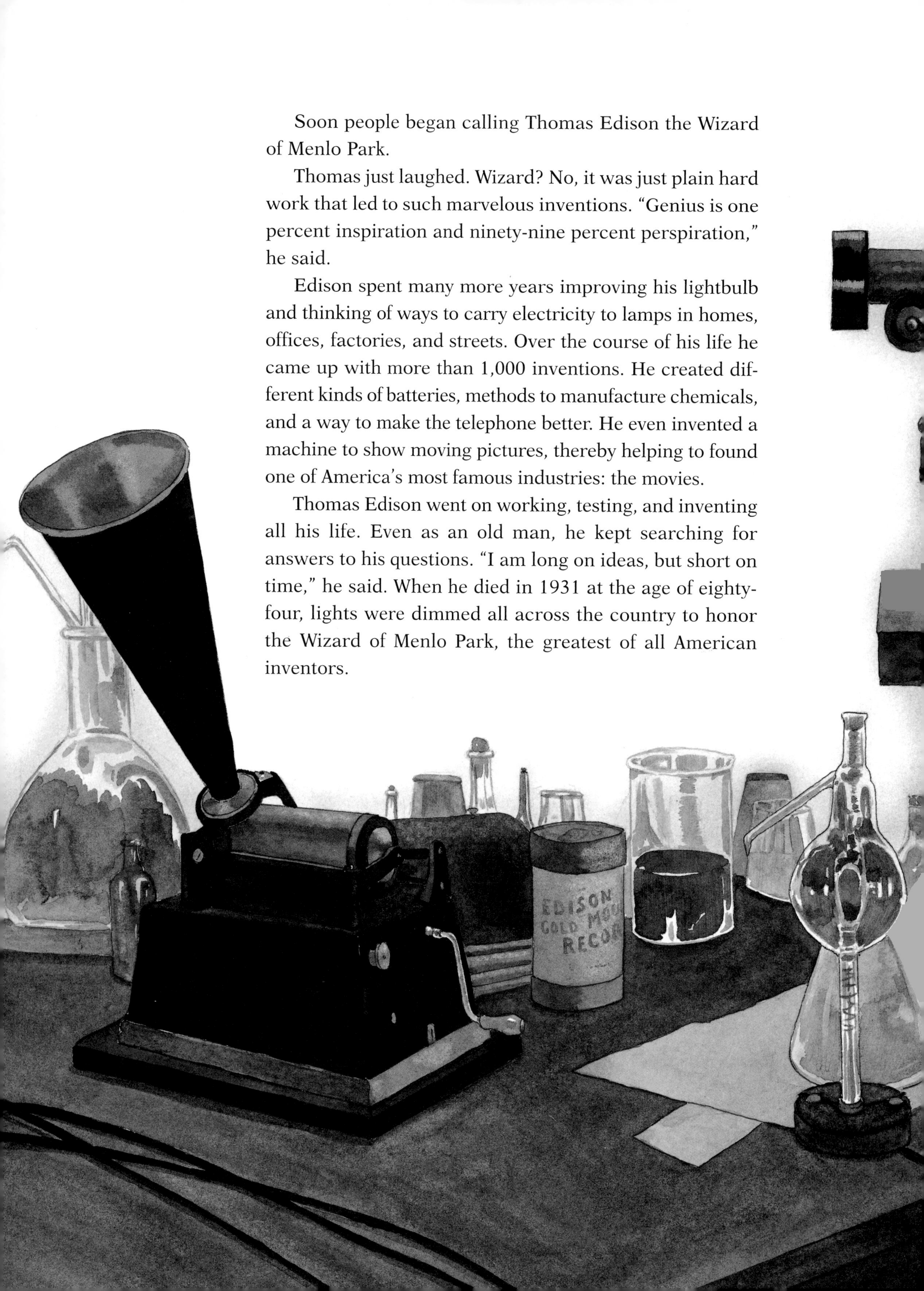

Martin Luther King's Dream

This is the story of one of our greatest spokesmen for freedom, a man who reminded Americans that all *of God's children are created equal.*

Martin Luther King, Jr., liked going to church when he was a boy in Atlanta, Georgia. His father was the minister there, and his mother led the choir. Martin's favorite hymn was called "I Want to Be More and More Like Jesus." He loved singing it while his mother played the organ. And he loved listening to the big words his father used when he preached from behind the pulpit.

"When I grow up, I'm going to get some big words, too," he used to say.

Home was just three blocks away in a big wooden house on Auburn Avenue. Martin felt happy and safe there. Every morning began with a prayer, and every evening the family was together for supper. Around the dinner table, Mr. and Mrs. King taught their children the important lessons of life. Above all, they taught Martin and his brother and sister to do unto others as you would have them do unto you.

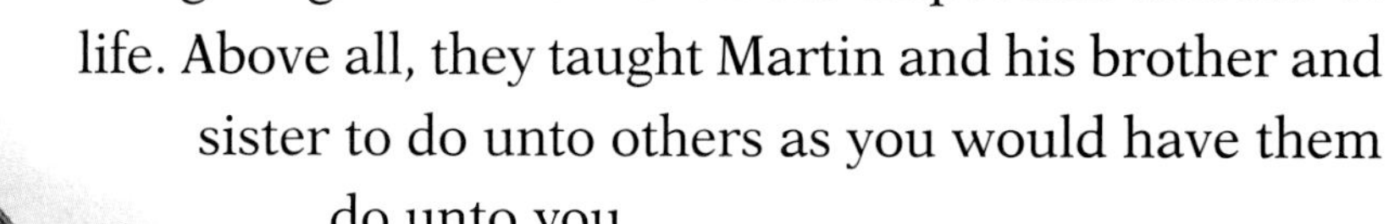

But not everyone lived according to that rule, as Martin found out when he turned six. That was the year he started school.

Two of Martin's good friends were white boys. Martin went to one school where all the children were black, and his two friends went to another school where all the boys and girls were white. After school, Martin ran to see his friends. But when he knocked on their doors, their mothers said his friends could not come out and play with Martin anymore.

"But why?" asked Martin.

"Because we are white, and you are black," came the answer.

Martin ran home to ask his mother why he could not play with his friends. She took him into her lap and told him how black people had once been slaves, and how Abraham Lincoln had freed the slaves in the Civil War. But in many ways black people still were not free, she explained, because there were laws to keep them from doing all the things white people could do. In the South, black people could not go to the same schools as white people. They could not eat at the same restaurants. Black children could not play in the parks white children played in or drink from the same water fountains. Blacks were kept out of many jobs, and in many places they were not given the chance to vote on election day.

It was hard for Martin to understand how there could be such laws. But he knew they were wrong. He told himself that someday he would try to change them.

Martin studied hard as he grew up. He liked words and books and the great ideas they could teach. At college, he decided to become a minister like his father and grandfather. That way he could help people be kind and fair toward each other, just as Jesus wanted. Night after night, he pored over the works of great thinkers and writers, soaking up their wisdom, and seeking answers about how to serve God and his fellow man.

After school, Martin moved to Montgomery, Alabama, with his new wife, Coretta, whom he had met in college. There Martin began his career as a preacher at a Baptist church, and there he found his chance to help change the laws that kept black and white people apart.

When black people in Montgomery wanted to ride a bus, they had to sit in the back, in a special section. And if the bus was full, the law said that the black riders must stand and give their seats to white people.

One day a black woman named Rosa Parks was riding on a bus. The bus grew crowded, and the driver told her to give her seat to a white man. But Rosa Parks was tired from working all day. And she was tired of being pushed around. She refused to give up her seat. The next thing she knew, she was under arrest.

Word of what happened spread quickly. All the black people of Montgomery were tired of being pushed around.

So Reverend King and the other black leaders came up with a daring plan. They asked the city's black people to stop riding the buses. And they began to speak out against the kind of evil laws that forced blacks to the back of the bus. It was a brave and dangerous stand. But Reverend King and his friends would not be frightened out of doing what was right. They stayed off the buses until the blacks could ride side by side with whites.

But there were still many other laws in many cities and states which treated black people unfairly. So Reverend King set about trying to change them, too. Across the South, he gave speeches saying that in the eyes of the law, all people should be treated as equals. He spoke in a rich, deep voice that made people stop and listen. Now he put to use all of those beautiful, powerful words he had read and studied. He used them to make people think about how they should treat one another. He told them he was speaking out because he loved America deeply and wanted all of its citizens to be free.

Again and again, Reverend King paid a heavy price. He received ugly letters in the mail and threatening phone calls in the middle of the night. Many times he was thrown into dark, lonely jails for giving his speeches and leading protests. Sometimes his heart sank, and he grew discouraged. But whenever he thought of quitting, it seemed as though he could hear the voice of Jesus saying, "Stand up for what is right. Stand up for truth. I will be with you."

One summer day in 1963, thousands and thousands of Americans gathered in Washington, D.C. Black and white people came from all over the country to call for a nation where the laws would treat all people as equals. They marched peacefully to the Lincoln Memorial, where Reverend King stood before them and spoke.

"I have a dream," he told the great crowd. "It is a dream deeply rooted in the American dream. I have a dream that one day little black boys and black girls will be able to join hands with little white boys and white girls and walk together as sisters and brothers. I have a dream today."

As the nation listened to Reverend King, people realized that the words he spoke were what America is all about: freedom and equality for all men and women, no matter the color of their skin. They realized that Americans need to live together, not apart. Across the country, more and more people both black and white joined Reverend King in his cause. As time passed, minds began to change. And slowly the laws began to change, too.

Then something tragic happened. In 1968, Reverend King traveled to Memphis, Tennessee, to help some workers get more pay. He was standing on his motel balcony, talking to some friends, when a gunshot sounded. Reverend King collapsed on the floor. In one brief instant, the man who helped millions of Americans find hope and courage was taken away, and the country mourned.

But Reverend King's dream did not die. Instead, people drew strength from his example and his words. Remembering his bravery, black and white people kept striving to make our country a place where everyone can work together, learn together, and pray together. They labor still to make it a nation where people of all races can sit down at the table of brotherhood together. Today all of us want the America of Reverend King's dream—an America where freedom rings for every citizen all across the land.

The *Eagle* Has Landed

Curiosity about the unknown led early voyagers to our shores. They called it the New World back then. Nearly five hundred years later, that same spirit led Americans to a more distant world—the moon.

It was one of humankind's oldest dreams. For hundreds of years, people had looked to the sky and wondered if they would ever walk on the moon.

"Never." Some shook their heads. "It can't be done."

"Someday," the dreamers insisted.

One July morning in 1969, three Americans, named Neil Armstrong, Mike Collins, and Buzz Aldrin, climbed into a tiny space capsule atop a giant rocket and waited for a countdown. Five huge engines thundered to life. Flames and smoke poured across the launchpad and Apollo 11 rode a column of fire into the sky.

"We have liftoff!" announced a voice on the ground.

No one knew if the men on board would ever make it back.

Gazing down, the astronauts saw the wide curve of the Earth with its spreading seas and lush forests and drifting clouds. Through the capsule's window, they watched their planet shrink into a blue and white sphere. The spaceship rolled and the Earth slipped silently out of sight.

For three days, the Apollo 11 astronauts hurtled into the blackness of space. A second sphere, this one gray and lifeless, swelled until it filled their window. Then they were circling the moon.

Neil Armstrong and Buzz Aldrin squeezed through a hatch and crawled into a boxy, four-legged landing vehicle named the *Eagle*. In this fragile craft they would try to drop to the moon's surface while Mike Collins flew high above, ready to rescue his friends if anything went wrong.

The radio hissed and crackled. A voice called from Mission Control in Houston, Texas, a quarter million miles away, "You are go for separation."

Slowly the *Eagle* and the mother ship backed away from each other. The lander floated free.

"The *Eagle* has wings," Neil Armstrong reported to Earth. Inside the cramped cabin, he and Aldrin watched the ghostly moonscape rolling by.

Everything was ready. Another order came from Houston. "You are go for powered descent."

The engine fired and the *Eagle* began its short downward journey. Armstrong nodded and Aldrin grinned to himself. They were going to land on the moon.

But suddenly bells began to clang inside the tiny craft. Something was wrong.

"Give us a reading on that alarm," Armstrong called back to Earth. His voice was suddenly strained. If it was a serious problem, they would have to turn back.

"Hang tight," came the instruction.

The *Eagle's* computer, which was guiding the ship, had signaled that it was having trouble handling all its chores. The astronauts' hearts thumped hard inside their chests. The gray face of the moon rushed toward them. There was nothing to do but wait for Houston to study the problem and tell them whether to keep going or abandon the mission.

Then came the command. "*Eagle,* you are go for landing. Go!"

The spacecraft continued downward.

Armstrong turned to the window to look for their landing zone. He did not like what he saw. They were not where they were supposed to be.

The computer was programmed to steer the ship to a flat, smooth place for a landing. But it had overshot its target. They were plunging straight toward an area littered with deadly rocks and craters.

A light blinked on the control panel. They were running out of landing fuel.

There was no time to waste. Armstrong gripped the hand controller and took command from the computer. He had to find a place where they could set down, fast, or they would have to fire their rockets and return to space.

Gently he brought the *Eagle* under his control. The lander hovered as Armstrong searched the ground below for a level spot.

"Sixty seconds," the voice from Mission Control warned.

Sixty seconds of fuel left.

Balanced on a cone of fire, the *Eagle* scooted over rocky ridges and yawning craters.

There was no place to land!

"Thirty seconds!"

Now there was no turning back. If the engines gulped the last of the landing fuel, there would be no time to fire the rockets that could take them back into orbit. They would crash.

The landing craft swooped across boulder fields as its pilot hunted, judged, and committed. Flames shot down as the *Eagle* dropped the last few feet. Dust that had lain still for a billion years flew up and swallowed the craft.

Back on Earth, millions of people held their breaths and waited. They prayed and listened.

Then Neil Armstrong's faint voice came crackling across the gulf of space. "Houston, Tranquillity Base here. The *Eagle* has landed."

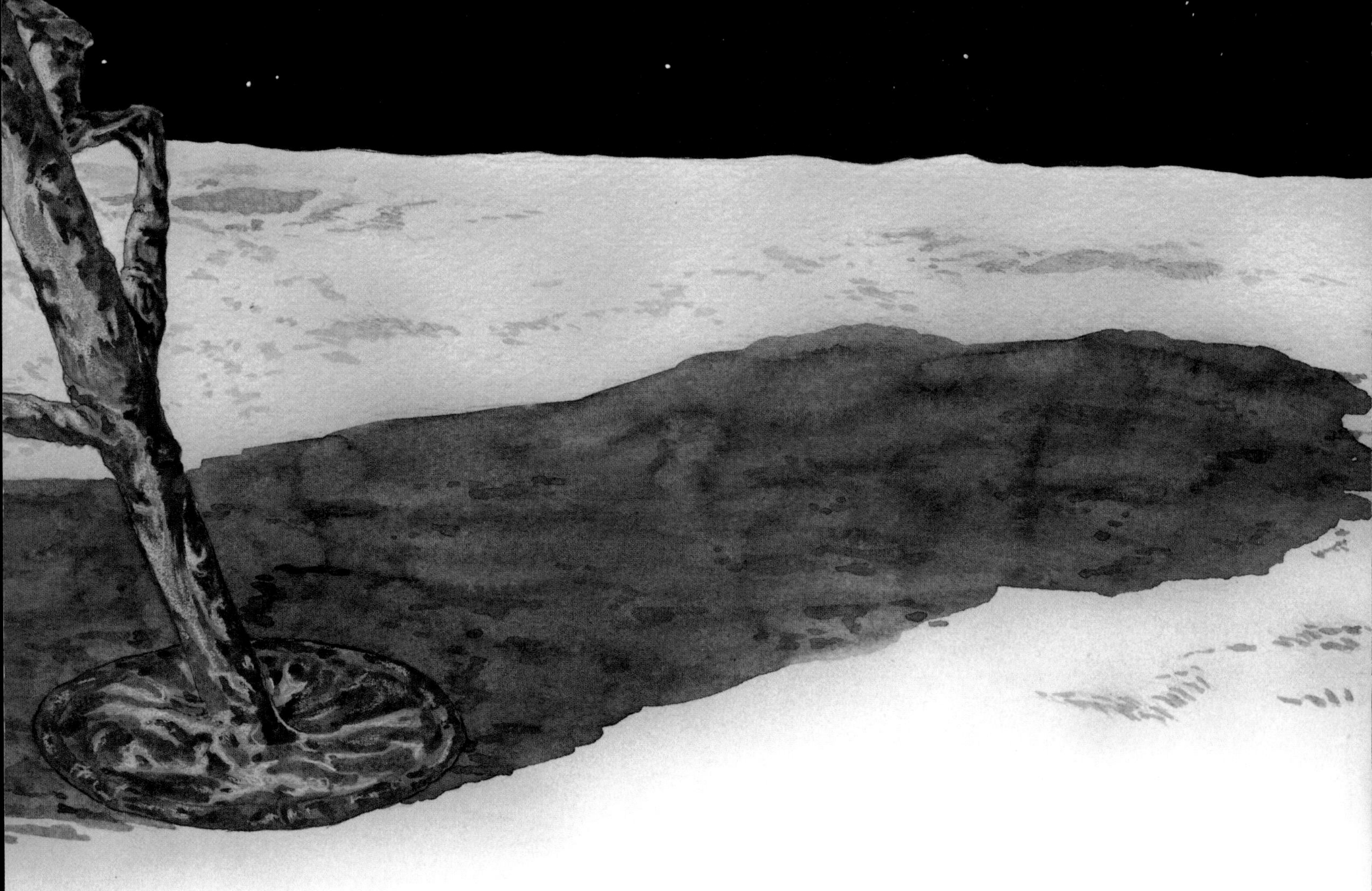

In a short while a hatch on the lander opened. A man in a bulky space suit backed down nine rungs of a ladder and placed his foot on the gray lunar soil. People all over the world watched the fuzzy black-and-white images on their television screens. They leaned toward their sets to catch the first words spoken by Neil Armstrong from the surface of the moon.

"That's one small step for man, one giant leap for mankind."

A few minutes later Buzz Aldrin crawled out of the *Eagle* to join his comrade. Together the astronauts planted a flag.

It would never flap in a breeze on the airless moon, so a stiff wire held it out from its pole. Aldrin stepped back and saluted the Stars and Stripes.

America had made the age-old dream come true. When they departed, our astronauts left behind a plaque that will always remain. Its words proclaim:

HERE MEN FROM THE PLANET EARTH
FIRST SET FOOT UPON THE MOON
JULY, 1969 A.D.
WE CAME IN PEACE FOR ALL MANKIND

"America"

— SAMUEL FRANCIS SMITH

A young man named Samuel Francis Smith penned America *in 1831 while he was studying to become a minister. "Let music swell the breeze," he wrote. Listen and you can hear sweet freedom's song indeed—God's American choir lifting their voices all across this great land.*

My country 'tis of thee
Sweet land of liberty,
Of thee I sing.
Land where my fathers died
Land of the Pilgrims' pride
From every mountainside
Let freedom ring.

My native country, thee,
Land of the noble free
  Thy name I love.
I love thy rocks and rills
Thy woods and templed hills
My heart with rapture thrills
  Like that above.

Let music swell the breeze
And ring from all the trees
  Sweet freedom's song.
Let mortal tongues awake
Let all that breathe partake
Let rocks their silence break
  The sound prolong.

Our fathers' God, to thee,
Author of liberty
  To thee we sing.
Long may our land be bright
With freedom's holy light
Protect us by thy might
  Great God, our King.